UNTHOLOGY 10

UNTHANK

First Published in 2018 by Unthank Books

ISBN 978-1-910061-53-4

Edited by Ashley Stokes and Robin Jones

Jacket Design by Robot Mascot – www.robotmascot.co.uk

Book Production and Typesetting by The Silly Spaceman

www.unthankbooks.com

Contents

Introduction

Fight or Flight

You know they are there. You just can't see them. You sense them in the bushes. Rustling. Rippling. Breathing. Brooding. They skitter in the shadows. One of them lurks in the coppice on the ridge. There's a face behind the face in the gnarled tree trunk. There's a man by the canalside watching for your approach. A woman will be waiting for you in reception who looks like the human form of blackmail. Someone else whispers that he knows of your lapses, your proclivities. There's an outline in the rain, a thin silhouette in the lightning flash. Scratches on the door spell out your secret in pictograms and hieroglyphics. At dusk, eyes will glimmer at the window. There's something under your bed that wheezes just before sun-up. There's a clown who wants your job and your house and your life. There's an old beast dragging its tail up your stairs. There's another in bed with your lover and you realise that your lover now operates under an assumed identity. Something lies across the track to upend your train. Someone put syrup in your engine. Someone is poisoning your coffee. They've done something to the air. Someone knows how much you owe and how much you've squandered. Someone has plans for you. Someone is living in your shed. Others eavesdrop from the attic. They buried something in the basement. They unearthed something in your garden and took it away. Someone stole your cat. They suggest that you should keep silent. Keep it shut, or you'll vanish. Someone thinks you're on the wrong side. Someone says you should kneel, submit. Some of them say you need to rapidly decide whether you are to be doomed, damned or doomed and damned. To which Circle will you belong? To what will you be complicit? Some of them say it was you who betrayed them. Some of them want to come here and squat on your chest. Some of them can travel through the ducts and crawlspaces. Someone must be reading your mail. One of them is signing you up for things that will only make it worse for you. Sometimes you come to in the middle of the night aware that you are no longer alone. They hide in the wardrobe. They walk the night in your clothes. Some of them look like the you that stares back from the mirror. The reflection that flashes by as you pass the shops is no longer you but a glimpse of someone else, someone who wants them to know you. Some of them say you used to long for authenticity but now you only hanker for escape. Some of them say you no longer know the distinction between decadence and degeneracy. Someone knows why you linger so long before returning home each night. Someone has been writing down your dreams. Some of them used to be your friends. Some of them swarm, some project. They all persist. Someone, you cannot tell if it is a man or a woman, is breathing down your neck. And the question, the question is, always, what to do now? How to act now that the catastrophe is here? Who do you want to be? How do you want to be remembered? A shadow of yourself or the self of your shadow? Fight or flight? Welcome to Unthology 10.

Rosa and Kelsey

Kathryn Simmonds

Matthew sits in the castle grounds checking his phone, an eye on his daughter as she muddles along beside the ruins. Early May and the sun is high at last, heralding the death of endless winter, brightening the view of sheep-pocked fields to a greeny blue haze.

It is his turn with Rosa. They agreed to split the childcare, which he knows is reasonable because his wife wishes to resume her career before it's too late, and yet he resents this yolk of restraining boredom. Of course he loves Rosa, but how long can a grown man sustain interest in the whims and wants and observations of a toddler? The trips to soft play centres, the negotiations over peas, the ever-present temptation to slot Maisy Mouse snugly into the DVD player; it all adds up to a banality he often finds overwhelming.

In London, his wife proffered leaflets for something called

Dad's Club, which he politely accepted and folded into the kitchen drawer. But here in the countryside there are no Dad's clubs. In fact, he's noticed few clubs of any description, though Megan has joined a pop-choir and does Pilates in the church hall on a Wednesday night. He watches films when she's out, and now the evenings are lengthening he kneels in their new garden to plant lettuces and carrots, remembering the seed packets of his childhood. The garden is part of their new life, one of the reasons they moved west, for space, for greenery and peace. But in truth there's only so much pleasure he can take from awaiting the appearance of a radish. In the city he had stuff to do. In the city he knew people. Megan tells him he'll meet people here too, it'll just take time. He hasn't told her the sorts of people he wants to meet are like himself and he's worried there aren't any.

In the distance his daughter carries a flat stone with extreme care, as if it's a cake she's spent all day baking.

Their friends in London assume they now inhabit some sort of idyll: country pubs and blonde beaches, teashops and county shows. On the phone, Matthew has allowed this. He feels it's no more than he deserves since these notions had already taken seed in his own imagination before the move: Cornwall, faintly golden in its rural glamour.

New voices drift over. Laughter. A group has settled at the edge of the sloping grass, five or six figures, a young man with his shirt off, chest tanned and hard-looking like the torso of a plastic Action Man. There's a dog too, racing in circles, one of those muscled breeds he doesn't trust. They're grouped beside railings where the grass stops, bathing in the first warmth of spring. Below is a steep brambled slope and then the road which connects to the A388. The dog makes Matthew nervous. He calls to Rosa and she pivots, curious, as if there might be a slice of dried mango on offer or a picture book, and lets herself be coaxed nearer. But halfway across the grass Rosa stalls: another toddler has wandered up and an encounter is in progress. Matthew observes. A quick scan gives the location of the girl's father, reclined in isolation beside a buggy, a can in his hand.

Rosa is socially confident. She knows how to form nearly complete sentences and writes an R with only a little guidance. The other child stands in her denim shorts, nappy poking out of the waistband, a dummy in her mouth. She makes a noise and the dummy spills to the grass. *Cuda* she says, arms open. *Cuda*.

Her father has risen from the grass. 'You want a cuddly, Kelsey?' He grins at Matthew and swigs from the lager. Sure enough Kelsey opens her arms wider and Rosa walks into them. The children embrace somewhat formally, like women at a wedding, before Rosa tries to work herself loose. 'Let her go, Kels,' says the dad, 'Come on.' He detaches Kelsey's fingers from Rosa's t-shirt. 'Wants to be everyone's mate, this one,' he explains. His hair is black like his daughter's, a shaggy fringe at the front, and when he pushes it aside his fingers are heavy with sovereigns.

'Tell the little girl your name,' Matthew instructs because

Rosa's usual proclamation is something of a party piece. She transfers her weight from foot to foot like an Olympic long jumper in preparation, and delivers a tumble of words: 'I'm Rosa Elizabeth Frances Wright.' Her white-blonde curls bob like ribbon in the sunshine.

'What'd she say?' asks the father.

'Rosa,' says Matthew. 'She says her name's Rosa.'

'That's nice, eh?' says the father to Kelsey, who is examining Rosa with mute fascination, blinking her long-lashes. The dummy is still on the grass. A pink smear stains the side of her mouth, lolly juice not wiped off.

Without warning the children decide to move. They circle one other, giggling, Kelsey collapses on her bottom, Rosa copies and they repeat the sequence of circle/ fall, overlapping each other with escalating excitement. The two men look on, Kelsey's dad still swigging, Matthew assuming a look of stiff contentment, hands bunched in the pockets of his lightweight trousers.

'How old's Rosa?'

'Two-and-a-half.'

'Right. Big girl.'

He asks Kelsey's age. Only two months between them.

'Ian!' One of the lads with the dog calls over. Kelsey's dad raises his can in acknowledgement.

'Dossers,' he explains quietly.

'Got any fags?' comes a shout from the shirtless one.

'Sorry, mate.' And then to Matthew, 'I'm not crashing my

fags on that lot, hardly do a day's work between them.'

The children continue to play giddily, squealing, chasing, and the men watch.

'You on holiday?' Ian asks.

Matthew explains the move, change of environment, how they want Rosa to grow up in freedom. This is both true and not true. Prices have driven them away from the city, good old-fashioned market economics, and when they looked ahead they didn't like the vision of themselves living hand-to-mouth in late middle-age, Rosa describing the skiing holidays of her teenaged friends.

'Manage the winter all right?' Ian's accent is local and he stands square, shoulders back.

'Just about.' Weeks of rain and everything shut, clouds of it drifting across the valley left to right, left to right.

'Some people can't. Don't blame them. Course, it's not often bad as the last.'

Biblical floods, collapsed railway lines dangling perilously into the sea like strings of fairy lights. Ian tells of relatives whose house was ruined, 'Water smashed a wall out.' Rotten floorboards, insurance delays. 'Did what we could to help, but it was a mess all right.' Matthew imagines Ian hefting carpets over his shoulder beneath spears of rain. There are advantages to being inland.

'Still, brightening up now. Bude weather soon,' he says, squeezing his now empty can and indicating the girls who are merrily rolling about on the grass. 'Those two hit it off.'

Kelsey shouts unintelligibly in their direction, and in the way of parents who must be their toddler's only link to the speaking world, Ian translates. 'Spongy?'

He crouches at the buggy and sorts through the basket. 'Rosa want one of these? Fruit biscuits, no shit in them,' he says. Matthew glances at the packaging doubtfully, but allows Rosa to accept with the usual 'Say thank you' ritual. Megan keeps a strict eye on sugar and additives but she isn't here. This is his watch. Rosa tucks happily in.

'Gotcha.' Ian produces a pink ball made of sponge and throws it to the girls, who give chase, biscuits in hand. Ian laughs, 'Her favourite. Goes everywhere – sometimes in her cot.'

Matthew smiles and wonders what sort of parents let their child sleep with a ball that's rolled over every dog-shit park and street.

'Takes it to nursery, too.'

'Oh right. Which one?'

'Kidzone,' says Ian, dipping into the biscuits and offering one to Matthew, which he declines. Kidzone. He knows the place, down by the tyre warehouse, a prefab space they toured out of curiosity. Three subdivided rooms, pay by the hour, girls who didn't look more than nineteen all wearing jeans and orange t-shirts with a smiling cartoon face on the pocket. A sandpit filled with dirty sand, no separate space for naps, a kid sprawled on a beanbag asleep.

'Kelsey loves it, wants to go at weekends.'

They'd decided against nursery in the end. Well, Megan had

decided. She believed children under three should spend most if not all of their time with a parent. She could quote studies. Matthew sometimes suspects Rosa would be having a better time in nursery than with him, but to admit this would be to admit his own shortcomings as a father, so he keeps quiet and they split things fifty-fifty: two days each and Friday with the childminder. Megan has made a couple of mum friends at toddler group and they journey to play farms together and local beauty spots. She returns home red-cheeked and exhausted, regaling him with tales of how the children fed lambs or ran down sand dunes. Always she is relieved at this new life they've decided on.

Kelsey appears and regards Ian with big eyes. 'Poop, dada,' she says.

'Oh fantastic, here we go.' He reaches under the buggy for a changing bag, whisks her up with one arm and throws her over his shoulder. He has the physique of a builder, or someone used to lifting and lugging at any rate.

'Gents are horrible,' he says, 'I'll take her over there.' He nods towards a copse of flowering shrubs, pinks and lilacs. If Matthew were better at nature he'd know what they were called. That was another image he cultivated before the move, himself striding about in hiking gear, an oblong map in his day-sack. Bodmin is a short distance, but whenever they've driven past the moors Matthew sees only a turfy expanse of wind-blown heather and he can't ever imagine wanting to traipse across it.

'I wear Peppa Pig pants,' declares Rosa, who has arrived at his leg. And then, troubled by the sight of her new friend borne aloft, 'Where Kelsey going?'

'It's all right sweetheart, you can play with Spongy,' says Ian, his daughter balanced on his shoulder and giggling as he pretends to take a bite out of her ribs. 'Back in a minute.'

Matthew encourages Rosa to play with the ball and while she fuddles about by herself, he checks his phone. He ordered a box set ten days ago, a cop drama he's only managed to read about. Must be a delivery problem – their lane is poorly signed and other post has gone astray too, his *New Statesman* and a clothing catalogue. Swishing at an endless Help menu he remembers an experiment he once read about: two separate boxes of rats are given a lever which dispenses dopamine. One box is bare, the other contains distractions. The rats in the empty box do nothing but press the lever. Tap, tap, tap. When Rosa is crayoning, he checks his phone; when he's heating lunch, he checks his phone; when she's playing fairies he checks his phone. The rats in the empty box die first.

Once he's re-entered his postcode for the third time, he glances up and there's Rosa kicking Spongy down the bank at speed. He calls, but on she skitters. It's safe, he knows she can't squeeze through the railings, but nevertheless he springs to his feet and bounds after her, shouting.

At the bottom she turns, the ball in her hands.

'Come here, missy!'

For a moment they stand motionless, regarding each other,

and then she raises the ball and drops it experimentally over the railings. 'No!' he shouts, too late. The blob of pink vanishes.

'Gone!' says Rosa, with thrill and wonder in her voice.

Matthew snatches at her wrist. 'Why did you do that?'

'Gone,' she repeats, pointing a dimpled finger.

'Because you threw it down there. That's naughty. It belongs to Kelsey.' He changes from a stoop to a kneel, aware he's pressing too tightly and makes himself release his grip. She holds her wrist guardedly to her body in case he should take it again. She blinks at him, 'Daddy go and get it.'

He sighs, assessing the ravine, the bracken. Daddy get it how? How was he supposed to scramble down there? A long circuitous path leads to the pavement but there's a high wall at the bottom, he'd still have to climb over.

'Naughty, Rosa. Very naughty.' He'll replace the ball, there's no other solution.

Now Ian is jogging towards them with his daughter on his shoulders.

'I took my eye off her for a moment,' he says, aware of a weakness in his voice.

'Down there, is it?' Ian swings Kelsey to his waist and leans over. 'Oh yeah, I see.'

'Spongey!' Kelsey whimpers, her face tremulous.

'Daddy get it,' Rosa explains.

'I don't know if I can, darling,' says Matthew gently, anxious to keep everyone calm. A tear skips off Kelsey's Disney lashes.

'It's all right, Babe,' Ian brushes her cheek with his square thumb. 'There's a gap,' he indicates to Matthew, 'through those trees. I'll go if you like. We used to chuck Frisbees down there as kids.'

Matthew assesses the clumpy overgrowth, feeling bleak. He must go. His child is responsible.

'Daddy go,' confirms Rosa, settling the matter.

*

His bare toes curl against the grainy insoles of his shoes for grip; at least he's wearing canvas lace-ups rather than sandals or flip-flops. But God, it's steep. He draws aside low branches, and treading with baby steps negotiates the first loamy incline. After only a few metres he leans against a young tree for support and assesses the way ahead. The ground feels loose and mulchy and from here it drops significantly, the trees become sparser and in among the weedy undergrowth are scribbly nests of root and bramble. He considers bumping down on his bottom the way Rosa travels downstairs in the new house, but he's too acutely aware of Ian watching from above, so instead he decides to run, to use the gradient rather than fight against it.

With another tree as his marker he forces himself from safety, his sights fixed on a branch which juts from its trunk like a crooked elbow. The slope rushes at him as he slices through shadow and light, his pulse banging high in his neck and in seconds he's at the tree, his chest slams against bark and he laughs involuntarily. What is this lightness? Adrenalin he supposes. Going back up will be easier – he'll grab the roots like a climber, use them as footholds. Suddenly he feels brave, alive, imagines himself telling the story to Megan over a glass of wine, returning to these images in his mind, himself as hero-father.

A voice filters down. He cranes up and there is Ian bending over the rails. 'Inside!' he calls. 'Face inside!' But Matthew doesn't know what this means and can't be distracted now, he has to concentrate, so he raises his arm in an 'All's well' gesture and turns away, back to the target pink blob. Thin traffic sounds rise from the road. Fixing his attention on the next tree a few more metres down, he takes a breath and plunges again, feet skipping and high-stepping, Fred Astaire of the undergrowth. The tree comes at him fast but he's ready and circles its body.

A bird clatters in the canopy.

He wipes sticky threads of hair from his neck. One more tree marks the next stop. *Come on then.* He gives a quick breath and once more rushes forwards, pushing into air, running down, down, through mulch and fern and root until – a missed beat, like missing a stair – his heart spills from its box and at once he's wheeling in freefall.

His descent is broken by a jagged stump.

What comes next is an ambush of pain. He is flopped on his side like one of Rosa's dolls. Foolish and swearing he hauls himself to a more upright position, and then, when his head has stopped spinning, raises his trouser leg. Nothing unfamiliar, the same flesh and bone, but now a new tenderness. He lies back and blinks as the twiggy sky settles above him.

Ian's voice again, indistinct. Matthew tries to raise himself. It hurts, he thinks simply. He can think of nothing but pain. 'Come down,' is all he hears. There's the sponge ball only a few feet below, round and pink as a baby's head. He tries shuffling towards it on his backside, which is at least more tolerable than putting weight on the ankle, but makes no progress and stalls, cursing afresh. And then movement from above and Ian is trampling towards him.

'You went down like a skittle,' he says. 'This ankle, yeah?'

Matthew nods, wincing, and Ian makes a cursory examination. 'Looks like a sprain. You've got to face inside, edge down slowly, keep your knees bent. I should have said.' The pain seems worse when Ian speaks. 'You need to pancake on the slope if you feel yourself go. Sorry mate,' he says, catching himself. 'Too late for that. I'll fetch the ball.'

Despite his advice to go slowly, Ian scampers towards the ball and back in no time.

Matthew thanks him. He doesn't feel like moving so he sits and Ian crouches. He has a thought. 'Who's looking after the children?'

'One of the lads.'

'What about that dog?'

'Pam? She's all right.'

'But you can't...' *You can't leave my daughter with those people,* is what he wants to say. He's pretty sure they were smoking weed. And the dog, Christ. The pain flowers at his ankle and climbs in tendrils the length of his leg. What now?

'D'you think you can make it back up?'

Matthew assesses the slope grimly.

'Here,' Ian swings an arm around him.

Step by step Matthew forces himself upwards, his path blurred by pain, snatching at occasional roots with his free hand, swallowing his moans. When he wants to stop he thinks of Rosa and the weed-smokers and the brutally muscled Pam, until at last they enter sunlight and green hurts his eyes.

The girls run giddy amid the dossers, chasing the dog. Kelsey throws her arms around Ian, delighted by his return and spongey's.

'Rosa!' Matthew calls, but she's engrossed. He limps towards her.

'Doggy!' she tells him.

The shirtless dosser asks about his fall, and Matthew replies as pleasantly as he can while encouraging Rosa to move away. The dog makes urgent snuffling noises as it plays, wanting the ball.

Ian checks his watch. 'We'll be late for your nan,' he says to Kelsey. 'Do you want a lift to the doctors?' he asks. 'Get that sprain looked at?'

Matthew thanks him but says he'll be fine, Megan's office is only a few minutes away. That at least is some comfort. Everyone and everything is only a few minutes away in this town.

'Come on then, Kels,' says Ian.

Believing they are all going together, Rosa follows, but when she sees Ian packing up the buggy and understands separation is imminent, she cries out Kelsey's name in distress.

'Kelsey's got to go home,' explains Matthew through his buzzing ankle. 'She's got to see her granny.'

'We come too?'

'No darling.'

'More playing. More!' A fat tear judders on her lower lash and spills. 'More Kelsey.'

'Cudda,' says Kelsey, opening her arms to Rosa.

'Tell you what, this is breaking my heart,' says Ian, reaching in his back pocket and removing a card from his wallet. 'Give me a ring, I have her on a Wednesday, they can have a play together. Give me a ring anyway, let me know how you get on.'

'Thanks.' Matthew takes the card: *Ian Abel, Painter & Decorator.* That makes sense – fit as a bloody mountain goat.

'I've got a couple of dad mates in town, we take the kids out. Lot less stress in a group, in fact it's a laugh. Some Friday nights we'll have a beer in the White Hart, few games of pool. Come along, they're good lads.'

'Thanks,' Matthew repeats, still holding the card.

'So, let me know about the ankle, yeah?' Ian rakes his black fringe.

'I'll be fine.' A warm ache is spreading from his toes to his calf. He can't be bothered going through the 'Say goodbye' ritual with Rosa. She sucks her fingers and watches them go,

Kelsey waving from Ian's shoulders. In a last ditch attempt to keep her new friend she makes a dash for Ian's leg and Matthew has to prise her messily away.

Through tears, he leads her to safe ground, away from the retreating Kelsey, away from the dog and dossers. He collapses and reaches for his phone to call Megan. Rosa can't give him the understanding he needs, she's too little, he knows this with his rational mind and yet it annoys him. How utterly self-centred toddlers are. She is fretting and grumping and her father is in pain, real and acute pain.

'Come and give daddy a hug,' he urges.

She frowns, suspecting his involvement in Kelsey's disappearance. 'No.'

'Come on darling, daddy's ankle hurts.'

'Oh.' The frown again. 'Kiss it better?'

She kisses his knee conclusively. 'Better now,' she declares, before remembering her list of grievances – wanting Kelsey, wanting Spongy, wanting another fruit biscuit. He tells her he can provide none of these. She opens her little doll mouth and gives a full-blown howl into the hushed afternoon. Too exhausted to intervene, he allows it and the sound seems to connect directly to his nerves. *Shut up shut up shut up*, he chants silently. After a minute or two he attempts unsuccessfully to pacify her from his semi-horizontal position.

Pam powers over with her mighty shoulders and Rosa runs towards her. Matthew can't make Pam leave.

'Get away from the dog!' he eventually shouts.

The shirtless lad approaches to call Pam off. 'She won't hurt, mate. Loves kids.'

Spent, Matthew says nothing. More howling ensues until he produces his phone and offers Rosa the only thing he knows will pacify her. Cartoons.

Blessedly, after twenty long minutes, his wife comes swaying over the grass wearing the sunflower skirt in which their daughter likes to hide.

'Mummy!' cries Rosa, and runs to be scooped up and kissed.

'So what happened?' Megan dips into her shoulder bag for a new bottle of water and extra strength pain killers. Her hair is bound up in a ponytail and she seems girlish and competent to him. He explains between swallows and Megan sits cross legged with Rosa in her lap eating grapes from a Tupperware pot.

'I watched Sarah & Duck,' says Rosa, keen to be included.

'Did you?'

'Only two,' says Matthew.

'Four,' corrects Rosa.

'It was an emergency,' he explains with a sigh. Rosa will need an extra day with the childminder this week, that's some relief at least. His mind spins off to the possibility of lying on the sofa in peace. Perhaps the box set might even arrive in time.

'And I played with Kelsey,' says Rosa, popping grapes into her mouth. 'I like Kelsey.'

'Oh lovely, a little friend for you. And one for you,' says Megan, reaching out to squeeze Matthew's arm. 'He must have been a nice guy to help you like that.'

Matthew shrugs miserably. 'What else was he going to do?'

'He could have left you.'

'He needed the ball back for his kid.'

'Oh don't be such a cynic.' She shakes her head. 'You don't believe that.'

Matthew doesn't know what he believes, the only thing he knows is his ankle and its furious throb.

'Mummy, Mummy, can I play with Kelsey?'

'She's gone to see her granny,' says Matthew.

'Tomorrow?'

'I don't know, love.' He looks away from his daughter's hopeful face, out over the fields to the sheep and their mindless grazing.

'Want to play with Kelsey.'

'I'm sure we could track her down,' Megan says. 'It's a small town. I'll ask some of the mums. You should have got his number,' she tells Matthew.

He shrugs and gives a noisy sigh. Her eyes are on him.

'God, Matthew. Just because someone doesn't read *The Guardian* or follow all your cultural references, it doesn't mean you can't be friends.'

'I know that.'

He thinks of the days ahead, all of them green, the months and years of green, Rosa growing up and away, and their flat in London with its galley kitchen and box room, the front door opening onto the beautiful, filthy city he has lost.

'You've got to make some effort,' she says.

'I'm in pain here, don't you understand? I'm in pain.'

'Sorry.' She leans over and strokes his head. 'Poor you. Poor daddy,' she says encouragingly, and Rosa takes him in with her round blue eyes and repeats the phrase absently before inserting a last grape into her mouth.

Ursa Minor

K. M. Elkes

They rose before dawn, morning-quiet, and loaded the car with fishing rods, backpacks and a tent, then drove out past their coffee shop and their bookshop and the bar where they first met, through quiet streets washed with rain (her bare feet on the dashboard, a map unfolded on her lap) and further, beyond the city, to glistening fields, red-painted barns, pretty 'maybe one day' towns and the green hush of the back-country, the heavy woods and low, wet mist; Jack and Carrie, easy together, on a road that kept climbing, through switchbacks and tree-darkened lanes, until they breached the clouds into a bright, clean, morning light.

They made these trips often, pilgrimages out of town that always felt as though they were going home. Jack had grown up on the rim of the suburbs, his street ending abruptly at a chain-link fence with open country beyond. Each day after school, he would wriggle through the fence, then canter up a slope ridged with high grass to prowl the woods above for wet-backed toads and copperhead snakes coiled like flower heads. Carrie's grand-parents, ex-west coast hippies, had a place in the Adirondaks where she spent wild, naked summers as a child, her skin turning from town-pale to mountain-brown, dreaming at night of climbing impossible trees and swimming among the quick, pink mouths of snapper turtles.

The first time they met, at a neighbourhood bar, it was this love of the wilderness that stuck them together like burrs. They swapped childhood stories, the strange joy-fear of being alone in the woods, the perils of witchhobble, poison ivy, skunk cabbage. How she would lie awake through summer nights listening to the tremolo calls of owls. How he had nursed a snowshoe hare found injured on the road, its fur glassy with frost. When they left the bar they were drunk and it was morning and both felt glassy, dazed and alive. They went for breakfast, then to bed.

Six months later they found someone who did wedding ceremonies in the national park and hired a school bus to take their friends up into the hills for the ceremony. Midway through the honeymoon Carrie declared herself broody and Jack said: 'I'm in'. There was an awed, thrilling shyness to the sex and to the talk afterwards about how many children they should have. It all seemed such a natural progression. Yet 12 months had passed without any sign of pregnancy. Give it time, they assured each other. Let nature take its course.

On this, their latest trip up into the hills, they were looking for a campsite tipped by Jack's friend Dale, who had taken his two daughters there once. But Dale had been vague with directions and they found themselves on a dirt road heading deep into the forest, then bouncing along a logging track, the smell of crushed pine needles filling the car.

'We could turn round, go back?' Jack said.

'No way,' said Carrie. 'I wanna see where this goes.'

When the track narrowed to a thin trail, they stopped. From somewhere distant came the sound of quick water. They unloaded their backpacks and set off into the forest. The day was warm and sunlight fell in hazy shafts between the trees. A track sloped down to the wide bend of a river, shallow over rocks. Further downstream, above an outcrop of mossy rocks, was a crude wooden cabin. It looked as though it was still in use - there was a good stack of cut logs on the porch, a couple of chairs. But when they reached the place it was clear no-one had used it for a while. The logs were tinged green and the paintwork had flaked liked dandruff. Inside it was bare, but the roof was sound and the shack was dry.

'Should we use it?' asked Jack.

'Sure. It's not like anyone else is putting it to good use.'

Jack cut a branch from a fir tree and used it to sweep out the cabin while Carrie collected wood and started a fire. At dusk the view was beautiful and they sat thigh-to-thigh on the deck, eating food straight from the can, listening to the call of loon birds above the river. When it grew dark, they tied flashlights to the roof beams with fishing line and made love on the cabin floor.

The next morning they were swilling out their coffee cups in the river when a bear stepped from the tree line on the opposite bank. Black with a crescent of blonde fur on its chest, it swang its head from side to side, sniffing the air.

They had encountered bears before, many of them, filmy with distance through binoculars or trotting away from a roadside as they passed. Once they spent an hour watching from a ridge as a huge black bear fished in a stream below. But this was much closer, the bear bolder.

Jack reached for Carrie's hand: 'Just keep still. It's not so big.'

'It's big enough.'

The bear paused, swung its head a few more times, then turned to face them.

'No,' said Carrie.

The bear rose up on its back legs, then dropped forward with a splash. It began to huff and its ears flattened. Jack bent slowly and picked up a couple of stones.

'Back away,' said Carrie.

'If it charges we'll scare it together,' said Jack.

The bear watched them retreat, step by step, the cups left to float downstream. Then it snorted twice before walking back into the trees, leaving the hush of the morning to settle again.

'Amazing,' said Jack.

'Yes," said Carrie. 'But it was too close.'

'It was just bluster,' said Jack.

'It was too close.'

They made their way back to the cabin. Carrie went inside, found the can of pepper spray and hung it from a nail by the door, then sat by the doorway, opened her book and began to read.

'I thought we could fish?' said Jack

'You go,' she said, without looking up.

Jack fetched his rod and found a spot upstream. He baited the hook and cast it, trying to settle into the familiar, smooth rhythm, though the river was running too fast, really, to catch much of anything. Through a long afternoon he listened to the wet chatter of the river and felt the heat of the sun arc across his neck, concentrating until he could no longer resist the urge to turn to the cabin and then the place where the bear had faded out of sight. But nothing stirred.

When he went back, Carrie was sat on the steps, wrapped in a sleeping bag. No wood had been collected. The fire was nearly out.

'What if I'd been pregnant?' she said.

'But you're not,' he said.

'What if we had a child, or children, with us?'

'But we don't,' he said, then spread his arms wide and looked around him. 'We know what to do. This is us Carrie. This is our place.'

Carrie nodded. Then she stood, headed into the cabin and began to pack. When Jack went in, she said only: 'I'm sorry. It's different now.'

In their kitchen a rash of penciled-in stars on the calendar showed 'good days for sex'. Carrie tried old wive's tales – raw eggs, hot sauces, grapefruit juice. She planted a rosemary bush in the garden and told Jack how, on the subway, she had sat in the warm seat left by a pregnant woman, just in case. Nothing worked.

Their doctor told them the next stage was analysis – Jack's sperm. On the delivery date the car's engine died, so they ran to the main street and hailed a taxi, laughing in the back as they rode downtown, the jar of semen kept warm in Carrie's armpit. The report that came back declared good motility and a decent count. Keep going, try harder, they agreed. But in the months that followed, sex became her sinking silently onto him, head turned, a clinical rhythm to the arching of her back. When it was over Carrie rolled away, slid a pillow under her hips and held up her knees to keep the hope in. And still nothing happened.

On the day of their second wedding anniversary, they made an appointment at the IVF clinic. Afterwards Dale called Jack: 'So tell me, what was baby-making school like?'

Jack described how the receptionist had smiled at Carrie, asked her for a few details, asked her how she was, asked her to, please, take a seat. And how, when the doctor called them in, it was just her name they used.

'This isn't your gig,' said Dale.

'Isn't it?' said Jack.

The doctor had a South African accent and was tall, balding, clipped. He explained each stage of the procedure. He gave Carrie sheets of paper with instructions and diagrams. He asked if she had any questions. Finally he looked at Jack.

'And what about you?' he said.

'And what about me?' replied Jack.

In the weeks that followed there were charts, timetables, instructional documents and how-to videos, sheets of pills, needles and syringes, appointment dates for blood tests. There was waiting in the emptiness of hospital rooms, hard plastic chairs and the rubber-soled quietness of nurses passing by. There was the same-sameness of hospital corridors and the high, clean, sterile smell of the place.

Carrie became engrossed in online IVF communities, where the women displayed strings of numbers and acronyms under their avatars – a shorthand for how many treatments they had undergone, the results so far.

'What's DH?' Jack asked, over her shoulder.

'Dear Husband,' Carrie explained. 'Saves writing a name each time.'

In bed, while Carrie slept, he sometimes thought of driving up into the forest, sitting for an hour, just an hour, listening to the night under a spilt litter of stars. He would drift towards sleep with the scent of crushed pine needles coming to him, the murmur of a river over smooth rocks until, from the corner of his eye, he saw a running bear, the angry shiver of its fur.

After the first cycle failed, Carrie said: 'I want to go again.

Straight away.'

And so they repeated the ultrasounds and the blood tests, the clinic trips, the same smiling receptionist. Process and routine.

'How you holding up?' asked Dale, as they sat in his backyard, watching his girls rise high on their swings.

'We're OK,' said Jack.

'Those IVF drugs,' said Dale. 'It must be tough for Carrie.'

Jack thought about how the times he had watched her pull thick clear liquid from tiny vials, then flick out the air bubbles like a trained nurse. How she balanced the syringe between index finger and thumb, then measured the hormones into herself. Sometimes, when she was out, he picked up the yellow sharps box and rattled it, wondering at the sound of dead needles. Once, she pulled out the needle leaving a black bubble of blood. He desperately wanted to put his lips to it and suck the droplet onto his tongue, to taste the altered chemistry of her body, but she wiped it away with a sterile swab and pulled up her pants.

'Yes. It must be,' he said.

He began to go to the gym. Twenty minutes hard aerobic work until the sweat dripped into his eyes then freeweights, pushing himself to one more repetition, then another. He enjoyed the iron heft of the weights and checked himself often in the mirror, the growing definition of muscles on his chest, the thickening neck and swollen veins beneath the skin of his biceps. But when he looked at the acned steroid users, Jack felt envy. He wanted that too, to inject bulk and rage into himself.

Afterwards, he would call into the local bar, order a beer and linger over it, laughing with one of the older women who worked there. Mostly he liked the way his muscles began to ache as he sat and drank. But the woman had deep, sorrowful brown eyes and wore her hair up in a way that made him feel good.

When the time came round again for his part of the IVF procedure, Jack went to the clinic and waited to be shown into a small, neat room. There was a sink with paper towels and a television with adult channels. Below it was a drawer heaped with magazines. He switched on the TV, turned the sound low and masturbated, watching a naked couple saw at each other, until he came, silently, into a plastic jar.

He was about to leave when the door opposite opened. He hesitated behind his door, then closed it quietly. After a pause the other man stepped out and walked to the end of the corridor . Jack heard a window slide open and the low voice of the embryologist on the other side. The window slid shut again and the man walked to other end of the corridor where the reception room door rattled open, then closed. Jack counted to ten, listened, then went out.

A few days later he stood by, while Carrie climbed into a chair in the middle of a surgical theatre, below a bright circular light. The two thick arms of the chair cupped her legs apart and a nurse folded the hospital gown up above her knees. The embryologist entered with the thin silvery tube of embryos. He sat on a stool between Carrie's open thighs and pushed the tube deep inside her. Carrie reached out for the nurse's hand and then it was over.

When the second attempt failed, Carrie broke the news to her parents, then asked them for the money to try again. When she got off the phone, Jack said: 'Should we not have a break? I mean, Jesus, Carrie?'

'My body,' she said.

Jack picked up his keys and drove to Dale's. He pulled up outside the house and saw Dale and his daughters in the front yard. Dale had the sprinkler on, chasing the girls round the lawn while they shrieked, hid and came back for more. Dale threw down the sprinkler and chased them both, folding one, then another under his arms and lifted them so their feet dangled, then he strode around the lawn, playing giant. When he saw Jack he lowered both girls to ground and waved. Jack waved back, then started up the car and drove on.

He went instead to the gym, deserted at that time of day, and worked himself hard, grappling with weights heavier than he normally lifted. He could see himself in a mirror, veins on his forearms and shoulders bulging and his face sweat-shined, teeth snapped together, a wild look in his wide eyes. He wondered if this was how he looked when he came inside Carrie, this straining face, the look of a man being slowly crushed. He let the weights drop with clatter of metal and wiped his face with a towel, pressing it hard over his eyes until it hurt.

'Wow, you were really going for it.'

He looked up. Saw the brown, sorrowful eyes of the woman worked at the bar.

'Yeah, too much,' he said. 'I didn't know you used this gym.'

'It's convenient. Plus a lot of good-looking men work out here,' she said.

She was wearing a lycra top and he could see two hard nubs beneath the fabric. They found a massage room that was unlocked and when they began to kiss he could taste salt-sweat on her mouth. She moaned and bit his ear as they fucked, but when he got close he remembered the image of his own straining face, the weights dragging him down and down until he felt himself begin to soften and faked his climax.

It was only afterwards, in the shower that he finished himself, toeing the slippery mess down the drain. He didn't rush home. Carrie would be on her laptop, sending and scanning messages on the forums, an old hand now, giving advice to the first timers. He found a new bar, knowing he could never go back to the old one. As he drank his beer he thought not about the sex, but only about the wilderness, the smell of the cabin, the swing of the torches as they made love that night. He thought of the bear by the river's edge, it's hard brown eyes. He thought of running towards it, shouting and the animal wheeling in fear. He thought of Carrie behind him, and her words 'It's different now'.

Weeks after the third visit to the theatre and the chair, Jack came home to find Carrie sitting in the kitchen, head down,

naked except for her bra, a neatly folded towel clamped between her legs. On the floor in front of the open refrigerator
was a smashed jar of pickles, and from the slick on the floor
rose the smell of vinegar.

She looked up: 'So it was closer, this time.'

He shook his head: 'Don't say it.'

Carrie's hand was pressed against her middle, as if she was
holding something in: 'I have my credit cards.'

Jack hesitated for a moment, the sour stink of vinegar sharp
and pungent between them, then went upstairs, pulled his
pack from under the bed, filled it with clothes and buckled
the straps. He went back into the kitchen, stepped over the
broken glass and pulled out some cheeses, a six pack, hot dogs
and bread rolls.

'Where are you going?'

He stepped back over the slick. The kitchen stank.

'I'd ask you, if I thought you would come,' he said. 'But you
can tell your friends on the forums what the DH has done.'

On his way out of the city, Jack stopped at Dale's house.

'I want to borrow your rifle. That .270.' he said when Dale
answered the door.

Dale, looked back inside the house, then stepped out onto
the porch. 'You don't hunt Jack.'

'It's just in case.'

'Of what? Maybe we should go wherever you are going
together.'

'Will you give me the gun or not?'

Dale sighed, then stepped back inside. A few moments later he brought out the rifle in a soft leather pouch. When Jack drove away, Dale was still on the step, watching.

Jack was shocked by how much the cabin had become overgrown since they had been there, how ferocious the process of nature. The roof sagged on one side and a sapling pushed its way through a broken board on the deck. A blush of ivy was reaching out across the side wall. Inside there was a dank smell of mould.

He set up a rod in the river, then gathered wood, dragged big branches until his muscles ached just as they did at the gym. He lit a fire, tending it until his face and hands were blackened. Then he cooked and ate a fat brown trout and drank a beer, and another and another until he began to doze. Then he crawled into his sleeping bag and slept a night empty of dreams.

Jack stayed for two days, fishing at the same spot, leaving his bait tin open next to him, eating granola bars and wedging the wrappers under a stone. On the third morning, he fetched the hot dogs from the food box and placed them on the deck. Then he unwrapped the cheese and put that out. He emptied out what was left of his bait tin, kicked dirt over the fire and picked up the rifle and his pack. He walked to a high point he had scouted the day before, up behind the cabin, where he had clear sight over the river bend and the shore on the other side. He wedged himself in between two rocks, on a little bed of dried pine needles and began to hum, quietly.

He waited all day until, as the sun began to sink into the long afternoon, the bear finally appeared. Its fur looked sleek and polished in the lowering light and when it stood on its back legs to scent the air, Jack saw the disc of blonde hair on its chest.

He shuffled down into a prone position, chest flat to the ground, legs spread, watching the bear the whole time. He inched the backpack in front of him and laid the barrel on top until it was steady. Through the scope the bear loomed big and Jack tried to slow his breathing. He knew the technique, aim low, squeeze don't pull at the trigger, place the shot where you want it to hit.

The bear hesitated at the water's edge, looked back at the trees from where it had come. He heard the faint sound of it huffing and the clacking of its teeth. When it looked back again Jack knew, with a quiet sudden understanding, why the bear had stopped. It was a female and somewhere among the trees there was likely to be a cub, clinging to a tree perhaps, waiting for its mother to return. Left alone, he knew the cub would be helpless, an adult male would eat it, or another predator, or it would grow weak and starve. It was only a matter of time. That was the way of nature.

Jack looked down the scope again, slowed his breath, waited for the breeze to still. He thought about what would happen when he fired, the rifle bucking and jerking in his hands, the spit of the bullet and its hot spin from him to her. The mother would shudder and die before the echo of the shot had gone and returned from the hills around them.

Jack tried to picture the cub, somewhere among the under-growth, listening, waiting. But instead a picture rose up of himself, meek and alone in the room at the clinic, the silent porn on the TV, tugging at himself and then listening for other men behind other doors, each holding their meagre jars, each hoping for life.

Rising up onto one knee Jack squeezed the trigger, sending his shot above the bear and above the river, above the trees and the mountains in the distance, above everything but the infinite sky and the roped clouds that slid through it. He fired again and saw the bear turn, moaning in fear for itself and for its cub.

Jack stayed on the ledge for a long while, then walked back down to the cabin, packed up and hiked out. He drove back, slow and easy, down along the switchbacks and the darkened lanes, down past the farms and the pretty 'maybe one day' towns, towards the lights at the the edge of the city, and on, to his wife and their home.

One for the Ditch

Brian Coughlan

In distortion my stare seems like an unfair reflection; stick-like arm and tiny bearded face. Then a dark presence looms into the scene. Plonked down. The creamy overflow meets dark wood, forms a pool around the base of the glass. I wait for it to fully settle; a slow process when you are as thirsty as I am – requires patience. The heavy black falling away, the white collar forming. It just takes time. As a means of distraction my eyes follow the activities of the barman, the myriad of little jobs; restocking the minerals, replenishing the ice, dealing out beer mats, re-arranging the bottles such-a-way; all the while that tiny crucifix around his neck falling and rising along its chain. I have no patience. My hand shakes; let it shake – for another minute or two – until the darkness has fully settled. Then a long relieving mouthful. It sticks to my moustache, tickles my nostril hair. I rub it off with the back of my hand.

There.

The barman: scrawny and mean-spirited. Placing a listing tower of pint glasses on the bar wipes the sweat from his forehead with a mangy old dish-towel. The same dish-towel is then used to dry glasses that have been held oh so briefly under a tap and rubbed with a dirty sponge stuck to the end of a stick. Very hygienic. As if having read my mind he looks deep into my eyes, the sponge clenched in one hand, a scum-filled glass in the other. He doesn't say a word; but I understand by his look, that if there is any problem from my side – if I raise so much as a mumble of dissent – I can fuck off somewhere else. He doesn't care one way or the other. I've seen him in full-flow. Best to stay on his good side, keep the head down. I do.

If not here then an empty house. A cold empty house with the same walls to talk to. All four of them. Sometimes they talk back. They say 'Go ahead. What difference could it possibly make?' Instead I drain half the pint in one long glugging mouthful. Bitter on the back of the tongue. Order another one quickly. Quick. The barman nods imperceptibly. Wait your turn. He places the half-filled glass on the draining board. Always have one ready to start before the one I'm drinking gets too low. What I like about this place is that nobody here gives a damn about you. They would rather look through you. They would rather pretend that you are invisible – so it's free to collapse here; to let it all hang out, well up to a point, naturally.

To go back to the empty house will mean having to cook a dinner. Then eat it. Afterwards clean up the mess. There is always a mess. Dishes and trays with grease. Which reminds me; I need to buy more washing up liquid. Ordinarily, after the dinner and cleaning up the mess – there is nothing else to do but turn on the television and be consumed by it – to forget the mess, especially if the mess has not been cleaned up. There. I admit it. Sometimes it doesn't get cleaned up. The mess. Always some football match on in here. It gives meaning to their lives. They wear replica jerseys and shout at the screen. *The players can't hear you. You know that, don't you?* Funny one. Apparently not. Nobody acknowledges the stray comment. Just stay quiet and watch the match unfold; as if matches really ever unfold.

My attention floats. I find myself gazing at the bar, at the hundreds of bottles of various colour and design and shape nestling together on ledges against a mirrored background. My reflection is right there, in among the mirrored glass, behind the bottles. I don't know what to make of it. Is it an ugly face or a handsome face? It's just another face, covered in a wispy beard. Every so often I adjust my footing on the pole running along the bottom of the counter and pull in my seat to allow people get past me without them having to bump into my back. I order another one, fish around for change in the deep seas of my pockets. Stand.

Standing makes me realise the need to piss so I negotiate my way to the toilets out the back. As I enter them, the urinals suddenly burst into life, fountaining onto the hard cubes of sweet smelling disinfectant. They provide me with something to aim at. I am pissing onto these cubes evenly and watching the resultant steam rise when from next to me I hear:

'Are you deaf or something?'

I turn my head, slightly. There's an older man beside me with spiky grey hair, features all smeared across his face in a big dollop of stupidity. Staring right at me he holds his tiny much-wrinkled trunk with two over-sized gnarled hands. It looks like a baby elephant's head. The whole effect. I try not to stare and don't supply a word to him. I'm completely lost for words. It seems neither the time nor the place unless of course you are tipsy and I am not.

'Are ya a bit slow on the uptake?' he says.

I go back to urinating and try to make it come out faster, much faster. He continues to stare at me. I can tell from the corner of my field of vision. When I'm finished, I pull up my zip and step back from the urinals to tighten my belt. Now he's gaping over his shoulder at me with a deeply furrowed brow, with one hand splayed open on the tiled wall, to stop him from falling down into the urinals, into the piss and the stink running for the hole in the ground.

'I'm talkin to you!' he shouts.

Seeing as I'm in a good mood I respond with:

'Shut your trap you dopey old prick.'

A mistake of course. I should have just nodded my head. Say nothing until you hear more. Instead I have now engaged with him. I can tell this, by the way he scrunches up his lips, and sticks out his head, considering how best to deliver his comeback. It's while washing my hands under the ice-cold tap water that he says:

'I don't know what it is – but there's something missing about you.'

I nod at him, in a good natured way and leave. He is still leaning over the urinals. Returned once again to my drink I briefly consider the strangeness of the incident and how pro-phetic his remark had sounded. The football fans have left; their scum stained glasses still sit on the counter. The barman has changed both age and sex into a young and extremely bored-looking woman. She leans against the register with her arms crossed, staring into space, doing nothing. With a nod to my near empty pint glass she drags herself to the taps and pours me another one. All the nuts are gone, I run my finger along the inside of the packet and lick the salt off my finger. I should really go, after this one. Clean up the waiting mess.

At the far end of the bar, he catches my eye, nods, his glass raised high in salute. I name him *Scourge*. Perfectly convinced that he knows me – from somewhere other than the toilet – *Scourge* nods again, gives me the thumbs-up. I watch helplessly as he waltzes and blunders his way indelicately through the crowded pub until he is standing right next to me, his twin-kling eyes raining down recognition. Meanwhile the bar wom-an wants her money. Her hand twitches with impatience as I sift through the coins. I think I have it exactly so I do the sum in my head, adding this coin and that to her palm as I feel her impatience growing and the dose beside me is talking into my ear and confusing my count. There, four sixty-five! And the hand closes on the money. Departs the station and arrives at the destination, jingle.

'Well, how are you keeping?' he asks, giving my back a good hard slap.

I tell him I've never been better. But there is a problem: either because I don't say these words loud enough or because he is deaf, I have to speak up: he bends right down to meet the words coming out of my mouth. It is such a pain in the arse to have to repeat something, especially something as inane as the last statement – but what else can I do? I hear the words coming out again but without any conviction. *I've never been better!* They are duly ignored. He is not here to listen; he is here to talk. And talk at me he will. I can see him getting warmed up. Taking a long draught of stout, I stare at our conjoined reflection.

'Haven't seen you ages,' he slobbers.

I try. I really do. I try explaining it to him – that I have never clapped eyes on him before in my whole life. We are strangers. I even go so far as to introduce myself and extend my hand. This attempt of mine is met with a blank expression and a phlegm inducing spasm that turns out to be his mode of laughter. He slaps me on the back again, harder than the time before. While wincing I am told to look down at his feet and when I do I see that he is not wearing any shoes. All he has on are a pair of thick work-man's socks. I can smell the fetid odour, wafting upwards, of dried-in sweat. It's like a mal-odourous cheese. Except worse because I can see the source of the smell, there's no mystery. Just his stinking socks.

'She hides them, to stop me from coming over,' he says. He's wobbling.

He extracts, from his trouser pocket an enormous handkerchief. Coins spill and roll across the floor as he unconcernedly rubs each hairy nostril of his big red nose covered in open pores. His two hands splay themselves on the counter. This is the lull period. His drink-soaked brain is trying to think of something to say. Instead he opens his mouth, teeth broken and missing, looks all around him – as if trying to figure out where he is. The hands pen me in. They do not look like they are made from skin and bone; they look like they have been hewn from over-dry concrete. A long inhale through those freshly cleaned nostrils. It's a bit like being slobbered over by a big dog, the same heavy panting and bad breath.

'What was the name of the song we used to sing?' he asks, squeezing my arm.

He is mistakening me for somebody else. Despite the impatient explanation it just doesn't register. I might as well be talking to the wall. The song we used to sing? His imploring look into my eyes, into the back of my cranium, yields no song title. I shake my head slowly and firmly, put my arm around his shoulder, push him away gently – as if expecting him to float gently away to some other shore. Instead the house-lights flashing dash him back against the rocks of my total disinterest. Behind the bar our old friend, the contrary barman, is slowly wiping his fingers on the dish-cloth and staring at me and my new best friend.

'He's not supposed to be in here,' says the barman, a steely look in his eyes.

Scourge noses his way under my armpit: the friendly old dog hiding from a telling off. I have to pull him out of there. Try and straighten him out. A silly smile all over his bright red face. Guilty by association – that's what I'm concerned about. I try and distance myself.

'You're barred,' says the barman.

A hammer blow. It catches him right on the kisser. He sways alright. Oh yes boy – I see his head duck down, a few beads of sweat flying off him but crucially, he stays on his feet, he doesn't go down like so many others would. He stays on his feet and not only that but he throws a haymaker of his own. He says:

'Michael, proper order now – you asked me to leave, and I did.'

The crowd in pub are tuned in to this statement. It comes from such a worthy and truthful place that it is greeted with an ironic cheer. Oh yes, and the knock-out punch is his gentle plea for one last drink. One for the ditch. Just a small one. I don't know the history between them but there must have been some kinship in the past, something unknown, because the barman turns and places a glass under the bulb. And a scoop of ice, a reluctant scoop of ice. Except now *Scourge* has no money to pay for his drink. The last of his change rolled away a while ago and has left him, bereft. Sadly bereft. The barman is already taking the drink away with a little scowl of satisfaction.

'Make that two!' I say and throw money for them.

No sooner has the barman doubled the order and taken my money than he begins grinning angrily; tells me to get him the fuck out of there. Who does this pup of a barman think he is? The dirty bloody pup. How dare he... I am winding up to begin my impassioned defence of the poor drunken man beside me when I feel him slump against my shoulder like a newborn. He drools on me and makes bubbles come out from his nostrils. Though still standing upright his eyes remain firmly shut. The responsibility is now mine to drink both whiskeys, which I perform in quick succession, following them up with a loud belch that elicits a cheer from the crowd. They give me unnecessary directions to his house. It is situated across the road, 'within spitting distance' I am told.

Outside it is neither warm nor cold. Just quiet, compared to the pub. Must have rained all night: his socks soak it up as I lead him across the road. At least he is capable of supporting his own body weight. I'll give him that much. I ring the doorbell, knock with the knocker. Nobody answers. There is nothing else for it – I take out my keys. Select the correct one from the bunch. Slide it into the hole. Turn it to the left and simultaneously nudge with my shoulder. The door opens. I leave him draped across a wicker chair in the patio room, mouth wide open, snoring softly. When I close the door after me his wife comes out, and devours the body – like an octopus that has been waiting under a rock – with her cardigan wound around her neck. All of her tentacles catching hold of its prey. I am already on my way down the hill coming close to the cathedral when I hear her calling after me:

   'It's cold, don't you have a jacket or something…'

I shake my head, keep going downhill. There's no point looking back. The cathedral bells will start any minute now and I want to be home before that happens. Before those slow painful gongs, before those awful deadened final gongs of another awful day, wasted. Anyway. There's still that mess to clear up, from yesterday and the day before. I should see to it before bed. Boil the kettle. Roll up my sleeves and get stuck in. Shouldn't take long. That's what I'll do when I get to the bottom. Clean up the mess. But then I am reminded: there's no washing up liquid. So it will have to be tomorrow then; at the earliest, I suppose.

Blowhole

Tom Vowler

Dear Mrs Stanley

Forgive me for writing, specially after so long. I remember the papers saying how you got so many letters, from all over the world, total strangers getting in touch and all, as if your business was theirs. Folk is queer, as my Preston says. I used to think how that's the last thing you'd want, that each one must sound the same after a while. Did you ever write them back? I suppose that would just encourage more. Mind, I suppose we is strangers, having never met, but I've thought about you so much, specially in the last few years, how we'll always have this thing connecting us, that it feels like we know each other. Preston says we ain't allowed to make friends, least not the sort who come round your house or invite you over for the holidays. Acquaintances are one thing, he says. Everyone needs them, to get by. Once, I got talking to the woman who runs the youth centre down the park here, and I got all warm in me tummy cos she was speaking like we'd grown up together or something. She made me a cup of tea and moaned about the kids being rude and stealing stuff, but I could tell she was fond of them really. It was just one of them nice moments, and I started thinking we could meet up and do stuff together, as couples, and I almost ran home to tell Preston about how lovely this woman was and how nice it would be to go out to one of them new places across town, get one of those fancy meals you see on the telly, then maybe see a film all together, not that I like many films, but going to the cinema is fun whatever you see, don't you think? But Preston said, You've got carried away with yourself, we don't need anyone else. Excitable is what he says I am. So now I walk a different way through the park.

I miss the town and all them people living there. Does old Cowley still run that shop in the market, the one with the little clowns that turn round on a pole? Like acrobats, they are. I used to watch them for ages as a kid, worrying they'd run out of battery or whatever made them go round. And Bobby's Fish and Chips, I bet that's still there, even though everyone knew he never washed his hands or changed the oil enough. Best scratchings ever, mind, if you didn't have enough for chips. My mam still lives there, down past the memorial, but I think my brother has moved out. I miss them so much but Preston says we can't ever go back, not even for a day, and so sometimes I ring her up and just listen to her voice until she hangs up. I think she knows it's me, cos once she cried and didn't hang up, and we were both just there, listening to each other's breathing for what seemed like hours, little sobs coming through the earpiece like she had a cold, and I wanted to tell her about our new lives here and ask her about the clowns. In summer I picture her in the garden, deadheading the roses, getting annoyed at the snails in her beds, but not wanting to hurt them. She used to put them in a jar and take them down to that bit of grass by the coal yard, and we used to tease her, saying they would crawl back, how they always remembered which garden they'd come from, no matter how far you took them, that they had little compasses in their heads. Sometimes my brother would go and retrieve them, and line them up by the back door just before she went outside in the morning, and we'd hear her scream as we ran to hide. Imagine that, a line of snails all staring up at you. When I first met Preston, he told me I should respect her more, which wasn't really something I'd heard a boy say before. He said mothers were the most important thing in the world, and that nothing would function without them. I was really worried, bringing him home with me that first time, even though dad had run off years before and I knew mam wouldn't be able to stop me seeing him. But they got on like a house on fire, chatting about this and that, how best to light the logs when they were damp, how to fix the upstairs tap what leaked, which Preston eventually did though it still leaked a bit cos although he knows about a lot of things, he isn't always good at doing them. He can be real charming when he wants, charm the pants off anyone, especially the women. Mam didn't even seem to notice how much older than me he was, or if she did she turned a blind eye. My brother never liked him, but then boys can get funny with each other, can't they.

I saw you on that documentary last week, the ten years on thing, and it brought it all back, as if it happened yesterday. You looked so much older, I mean more than how someone would after that long. Sorry, that sounds rude and all. I'm no spring chicken myself now, although Preston says I'm still more beautiful than any girl he's ever seen, which is why I'm not allowed to dress all tarty, as it gives men the wrong idea and then they think it's OK to come over and talk to me, try to buy me a drink. Only want one thing, he says, so best not to encourage them. When he's out nights catching rabbits or fishing, I go upstairs and open the box of clothes hidden under the bed, things I've bought in charity shops, real pretty stuff that some elegant women must have given them, a long open-backed dress, a silk scarf that I try to make look nice but it never sits round my neck right. I pretend we're going to a ball or some big party, where all our friends are drinking fancy wine and passing round trays with those small pastry things on, and couples are dancing or playing party games. I tie my hair up, put some make-up on and a few pieces of jewellery Preston let me keep, and I walk all sophisticated round the bedroom, pretending to talk to everyone, who all laugh at my jokes, which ain't really funny, but it don't matter cos we're all friends and nobody judges us.

You looked so tired on the telly, as if you needed a really long sleep. You still have the same dog, I see. Or is it a different one? We have a Jack Russell, which Preston takes out rabbiting. It bit me once, so I didn't feed it for several days. Not that I told Preston, he loves that animal more than anything. I want to get a cat, but it wouldn't last five minutes with those two. Did you have any more children? The man on the programme didn't say. I shouldn't ask, I suppose. Me and Preston don't have any. He says it's my fault, that my insides don't work properly, but how would he know? Perhaps he's the one what's broke. I get sad, knowing I won't be a mam. Sometimes I follow the pretty women along the seafront as they push their prams, making sure they don't see me looking, or if they do I pretend I'm one of them, tell them mine is at nursery, which if I say enough times I believe it myself. Sometimes they let me put my hand in the pram, where if I'm lucky I'll get a finger squeezed and a big gurgling smile, although one woman started shouting at me when I kept my hand there too long, and I tried to calm her down but there's no helping some folk. Did I say, we live by the sea now, one of them little terraced cottages with a pretty garden? Each year a bit more of the coast falls into the sea, so nobody can sell them now. Our landlord tried to put the rent up last year, but Preston stood firm, told him no one else would live here, what with the damp. It's the salty air apparently. If you walk out on the headland, it's like you're on an island, and there's this blowhole you can stand by at high tide, and if you're brave enough you look down in it until the last minute, the water explodes out and drenches you and your face tastes of the sea. Mostly though I just pick flowers along the path there. Apart from the wood burner, the house isn't heated, so we snuggle up under a blanket with the dog on us. In winter Preston takes the truck out nights, fills it up with logs from people's yards or from the pubs out on the moors. He got caught once, I think, cos the police came round, but nothing happened. I mean how do you prove a load of logs are someone else's? I tell him we should be grateful for what we've got, that we don't need to thieve stuff. I suppose everyone wants a little more than they have. He doesn't know I'm writing this, he'd probably get one of his rages on. He's better than he used to be, but when that red mist comes over him. The first time I seen his meanness was down by the allotments, you know, the ones off Cecil Street? Our dad had one before he ran off, nothing fancy and not that he grew anything, just went there to get away from mam. Used to just sit in his chair, watching the day go by. We used to go down there in the afternoons, when it was quiet, have a smoke and drink whatever Preston had taken from home. He told me he had something to show me that day. Like a present, I said. Yes, like a present. I was supposed to be in school still, but Preston said teachers had nothing to learn me that he couldn't. They wrote my mam, but I think she just gave up in the end, short of marching me there and tying me to the desk, there was nothing could be done. I wish

I had gone to classes a bit more though. There's a library few streets from here, a poster in the window saying free computer lessons, and I tell myself I'll go in and ask, and learn stuff about the world, so I can better myself and come home and impress Preston, but I never do. That sounds funny, don't it, impress Preston.

It was raining that day at the allotments, big fat drops like someone had torn a hole in the sky, and I remember slipping on the ground and Preston laughing at me, at the mud all up my trousers, and I laughed too but really I felt like crying, sat there in the mud, looking up at him as he grinned and swigged whisky. We walked down the paths, and every now and then Preston would jump onto a vegetable patch and start pulling up everything, potatoes and parsnips flying through the air, swedes he liked to play football with, onions which he'd throw at me. Sometimes there'd be shouting from across the other side and we'd have to run till my sides hurt and I couldn't breathe anymore and Preston would tease me, tell me he'd leave me behind one day, and that perhaps I wasn't cut out for the sort of life he had in mind for us, which apparently would involve a fair bit of running away. We walked to the far corner that day, where there were some sheds, and I could see he'd broken into one from the back, a hole just big enough for a small person to get through, which in those days he was. I was glad to get out of the rain, and Preston lit up a couple of cigarettes, passed me one and told me to sit down. Want some, he said passing the whisky, and I pretended to take a big mouthful, but didn't really, although the fumes alone made me cough, which he thought real funny. Watching him then, the rain dripping off his fringe, smoking hard like some film star, it was the first time I knew I really wanted him, and despite what happened I let him have me later that night, in my room, hoping my mam and brother were asleep. I remember wondering, apart from the pain, what all the fuss was about. Still wonder even now, if I'm honest, and I'd like to say it doesn't hurt like that first time, but sometimes it does. Afterwards, I cried a bit, told Preston I loved him, saying it beneath my breath so he couldn't hear, cos he don't like talk like that.

That day, in the shed, he picked up this hessian sack from the corner, its top tied with a boot lace, and placed it by my feet, the bag moving a little from inside like it had a will of its own. Open it, he said, and my heart pounded away like a good 'un and I didn't know whether to be excited or afraid. Go on, he said, it won't bite. The knot was tight but I got my nail in behind it until it loosened. There was this awful smell that made me gag, worse than the whisky, don't mind if I never smell it again in a hundred years. At first, cos the rain had made it dark, I couldn't tell what I was looking at. The cat stared up at me, real scared, and I wondered why it didn't try to get out, but then I saw its legs was all limp, and that it weren't well at all, and I thought how nice that Preston had rescued it, even though there probably wasn't medicine in the whole world that could fix it. Can we keep it, I said. Course we can't keep it, he said. It's a stray. Probably got fleas. Best put it out of its misery. He picked the bag up, looking at me all the time, telling me to stop crying, which I didn't know I was. I hated the noise it made, or the lack of noise now I think about it, when he brought that spade down again and again, but I think it was the best thing to do, not that I could have done it. Later, after I'd let him have me, I wanted to ask about its legs, where he found it, but I didn't. I guess meanness just gets passed down. Preston told me once his father used to make him take a bath before caning him, so his skin was softer.

Do you still see your husband? The telly said you ain't together anymore, which made me sad. To go through all that and then to lose each other. It's weird, but I guess in some ways it keeps me and Preston together. It's not like there's anyone else we can turn to, or tell. I still love him. He was my first, so I've nothing to compare it to, but we're happy in our own way. He's had others, a couple since we met that he thinks I don't know about, and there's this girl two doors down that looks at him like she'd let him do anything, and I can tell he wants to. Will you have more children one day? Perhaps you're too old now, though I read somewhere about a woman in her fifties, which is a bit disgusting when you think about it.

I wish Preston had stopped after the cat, so we didn't have to move away. Sometimes I hope they'll find us, bring us back, even though it means never seeing Preston again, leaving the cottage behind, never looking down into the blowhole again or picking flowers on the cliff path. Would they let me see my mam and brother one last time, do you think? Preston says he'd go down fighting. Not built for prison, he says. Don't suppose I am neither. He isn't a bad person really, he just goes too far sometimes.

I should go now, get this in the post before he gets home.

From,
Susie

Cafeteria

Jay Merill

There is a woman with a bitemark on her cheek. My mother says her name is Mary. She is a prostitute. When I was first told this, by a girl from my school, I didn't know what it meant. But the girl made a bad face as she said the word so I knew it was something horrible. If this woman appears down the street all the other women out there walk away fast and don't seem to see she's coming. My mother stops, says hello to her. This makes me shudder but at the same time I feel proud. The woman is chubby and wears a red dress with laces at the front, and tassels. The dress has a sleazy look to it. When I know what the word prostitute means I imagine her being unlaced for use. As if she is a shoe which a foot is expected to enter. Girls from school whispered she went with sailors. I thought of the cheek bitemark, imagined sailors wrapped in wolfskins leaping up. And maybe she was a wolf too and the dress only a disguise. Something aggressive about the bitemark made me think so. Yet prostitutes had sex for money I now knew. So maybe she was not a wolf. Wolves would tear the flesh off you strip by bloody strip. Wolves do not need to ask for money.

I went on the bus with my mother to the Botanical Gardens. We walked along the graveled paths, the grass had a slippery look because it had been raining. It was not raining now but there were puddles. I stared down into the deepest puddle I could find to see reflections of the trees and of myself. When I looked up again I saw the prostitute just ahead of us. She was walking in our direction. She wore a loose jacket with a fur collar and spiky plastic boots in which she tottered. Looking as though at any minute she might fall. Her lipstick was brightest orange and had gone all smudgy, extending well above the line of her upper lip. And when she stopped to smile at my mother and me you could see traces of it on her teeth. She had a little boy with her. My mother said it was her son. He looked sullen with a baby-face. I hoped I wouldn't have to play with him. I crouched down and stared into the puddle at the reflected trees. They were swaying because there was a gust of wind. My mother was talking to the prostitute and this went on for a long time. I tried not to see the boy who was standing nearby kicking at loose stones on the walkway. Next minute it started raining. Telltale drops were splashing on the surface of the puddle. I was glad because I wanted to go to the cafeteria and now Mum would say goodbye to the prostitute in a hurry and take me there. When I looked at her I saw that the woman had something running down her face. At first I thought it was the rain. But there was a noise coming from her too. A strange dry howling that unnerved me. I thought of wolves at once and wondered if after all she was one. Then I saw she was only crying. My mother opened her handbag and fished out a packet of tissues.

'Here,' she said.

'You could do with a coffee,' I heard my mother saying next and she took the lady's arm and turned in the direction of the cafeteria. I followed suite but the boy did not move. He stood in the sudden fast rain until the prostitute had called him three or four times, her voice becoming screechy. Then glum faced he tagged along behind.

We got inside, rain splattered, shaking out our hair, the woman now laughing not crying, the boy with a blank look. My mother spotted an empty table over by the window, told me to go on ahead and keep it for us. I hoped the boy would not come with me. He did not. It had got very crowded because of the downpour and I sat there for what seemed like ages before I saw the three of them coming along a suddenly formed gangway on the polished floor – I thought of an ocean, the waves dividing miraculously so they could pass. But no, the truth was more that the people were giving them a wide berth to let them through quickly. As though the three of them were poisoned and the rest might catch something if they let them get too close.

Our table when they reached it seemed strange, like a lonely island cut off from the mainland by a stretch of sea. It had gone quiet at the tables on either side. There was some nudging and giggling and any number of filthy looks. But everyone had stopped speaking. Pointedly. My mother handed round some sandwiches she'd bought and took no notice. I couldn't tell if she was aware of the awkwardness or not. To me our table had a special glowing look. Both contaminated and pure. We were set apart.

I felt ashamed and angry as I sat there. I watched the heaving breasts of the prostitute in fascinated horror. The loops of her dress were taut as though she was starting to burst out. She sat right opposite me and was crying again. Then she took a gulp of coffee. My mother was right. It seemed to do the trick. Mary dried her eyes. The boy looked expressionless, the same as before. All at once my mother opened her bag and took out a packet of Smarties. She handed them over and he stared and stared as though he'd never seen such a thing in his life. A bit of dribble slipped from the corner of his mouth.

'What do you say?' the prostitute said to him.

He didn't utter a single word and seemed to be in a trance as he swallowed down sweet after sweet without a pause. All the colours together, he didn't seem to care which went with which. They were my sweets and I felt a bit aggrieved that he'd had them and without even saying thank you on top of that.

The prostitute started smiling at me, the bitemark quivering. I felt hotly embarrassed and wished I could run away or hide underneath our island-table. Or even die right there. But also

I felt strangely elevated and glad to be a part of this special cut off hellish place that my mother had introduced me to. I looked over at the people at the ordinary unspecial tables. They were the wolves if anything, menacing, huddled tight together in a pack.

When we were going home on the bus my mother said she'd get me some more sweets and was pleased I didn't make a fuss as that would have been unkind. She said there was something the matter with the boy and it was very sad.

Tenth Circle

Liam Hogan

I flick through the thick stack of parchment, skimming rather than reading, but it's enough to get the gist.

'Dante, Dante, Dante,' I say, slowly shaking my head. 'It's a bit… dark, don't you think?'

His Adam's apple bulges and his hooded eyes widen just enough for me to take in his startlingly blue eyes. He claims to be descended from the Ancient Romans, but perhaps it has mixed with other blood over the centuries. His gaze scurries away like a nervous rabbit and when he looks back the blue is hidden, his eyes narrowed down to slits. 'It's allegorical-'

'All this stuff about hell. Dark and gloomy. You call this a comedy? Even if you can get people to read an epic in verse form, it's not exactly much fun. Hard work, you know? Peg it back a step, Dante my son.'

He shifts in his chair. I'm hardly surprised; there's only one comfortable seat in the monastery's austere office and he's not the one sitting on it. 'It's the first part of three-'

I bury my head in my hands and he, thankfully, shuts up. 'A trilogy, Dante?' I say wearily. 'There's no point writing a trilogy until you know the first book will sell. And this, I'm afraid, won't.'

I tap the front page, the ill-written title. No scribe, our Alighieri. 'And you can hardly call it a Comedia. Inferno's okay I suppose, quite catchy, but you'll have to drop the Dante. You need to be well known before you can name a work after yourself and you need to be very well known before I'll publish a damned trilogy.'

He peers over his hawkish nose. That bit of him at least is undeniably Roman. 'I am well known.'

I sniff. 'In Florence, maybe…' I push the manuscript further to his side of the desk.

'What shall I do with it?' he asks after a moment's pause, finally grasping the meaning of my action.

I stroke my chin. 'Well, you could take it to Saint Augustine's and ask for Friar Abrahams. They like their gloomy religious stuff over there. Though, I do warn you, they also tend to burn people at the stake if Christian dogma isn't strictly adhered to. So they might baulk at ten different types of hell. But really, is it worth it? Why don't you try something lighter, in prose form maybe? People are big on prose at the moment. Target it at someone. Imagine that person reading it, or you, perhaps, reading it to them. And write about what you know, yes?'

Humbled, he picks up his manuscript, fiddles for a moment with the cord it was bound with when he arrived and then abruptly leaves, a flurry of unnoticed pages falling just as he closes the thick wooden door.

I ink my quill, jot a note in my ledger, and then call for Brother Alfredo, to clean up the spilled sheets and send in the next wannabe writer.

*

Six months later, Dante sits before me again, grinning like a loon. I surmise he has taken too much ale at the nearby inn; the potent mead is monk-brewed and the resultant glazed look I have seen many times before, even, on the rarest of occasions, staring back from the tepid water in my washbowl.

I thumb dejectedly through the sheaf of papers, almost as thick as the first. Has he taken any of my advice on board?

'This is still verse, Dante.'

'Yes,' his smile widens. 'Paradiso! I have dedicated it to Beatrice.'

Perhaps he has been sitting in the noon-day sun as well as quaffing the local ale. Though he has the pallor of a man who confines himself strictly to his cell, even in the middle of this unexpectedly pleasant summer. And who is this Beatrice, I wonder? Has the hook-nosed Alighieri a bit on the side?

Reluctantly, I skim the grandiose text. 'Only nine heavens, Dante? Shouldn't there be a tenth?'

His inane smile falters for a moment. 'I... mislaid one of my hells.'

I recall his hasty departure, the flurry of lost paper, and sigh. 'You don't quite get it, do you Dante? Okay, so it's not quite as much doom and gloom, but Heaven? Do you really hope to convince your readers you've had a personally conducted tour? And what's next, Purgatory?'

His frown deepens and he lifts an ink-stained finger to his lips, chews at a nail. I feel a flood of sympathy for the poor deluded man. 'Let me show you something,' I say.

I open the door at the back of my office. A half-dozen steps below, a cloistered square stretches before us where small desks are packed in tight. The only sounds are the scratching of pens and the occasional consumptive cough.

'One hundred scribes,' I say softly. 'All working on a single book. A guaranteed bestseller, as I personally know the buyers of each lovingly transcribed and illustrated folio. Our biggest print run this year: twenty-four copies.'

It's an awe-inspiring, glorious sight and I'm glad it impresses Dante so. This, after all, is what he is dreaming of: this is publishing success in all of its majesty.

I give him a moment to take it all in. 'Now, if you look over to your left, by the corridor, you'll see a discarded stack of sheets.' I point, and his sleepy eyes follow. 'Mistakes. Misprints. Not many, as my scribes are the best there are. Some of these sheets we manage to scrape clean, the price of vellum being what it is. Those that have already had that treatment and will most likely fall apart if we attempt it again... well. The corridor leads to the privy and I won't be so indelicate as to say why the stack is at its entrance.'

He frowns and I can tell he's about to ask why I'm showing him this. So I let him have it.

'That pile is also where unsold copies of books end up. Pulped. Remaindered. And I think, heck Dante, I know that you really don't want my monks wiping their bony arses on your work, do you?'

He rears back, shocked, shakes his head vehemently and I quickly raise a finger to forestall his inevitable burst of outrage and so protect the innocent ears of my younger scribes.

'Think about it Dante. Think about what the audience of today actually wants to read. Make it real, and true, and funny, and, if you can, sexy. You're not writing for your immortal soul, you know. You're writing for an elite audience, a privileged and usually rather bored one. Entertain them, Dante. Bring me something exciting, something new, something now, and I'll print it.'

I shrug. 'Maybe not a twenty-four-book run, maybe only a half-dozen, initially. But you work with me and I'll bust a gut to make sure none of them ever end up at the privy door. Can you do that, Dante my son?'

He nods, uncertainly, and I lead him back to my office, where he gathers his papers once again and leaves, head bowed, deep in contemplation.

*

I don't spare old Dante another thought, not for almost two long years; until one wet spring morning when Brother Alfredo bursts into my office cradling something large and leather-bound in his hairy arms.

'Master!' he cries, 'It's Dante! He's only gone and created a masterpiece. A bloody masterpiece! Everyone's saying so.'

Brother Alfredo is not cut from the same cloth as the rest of my scribes, a fact I make good use of when attending book fairs. Handy in a ruck, he also always seems to know where the best after-parties are.

I turn the freshly written pages, curious, expecting some ribald text of sex and intrigue in Florence high society, wondering why the ingrate didn't bring it to us first, given it was I who put him onto the right track. But no, it's the same old verse with the same dreary beginning. The bound volume is massive, I'm amazed even Alfredo could lift it. Here is Heaven and Hell spliced together with – and I have to laugh – Purgatory, all three parts combined in a single tome. I scan for a publisher's name, but can't find one.

'Self-published ...' I curse. 'A masterpiece, you say?'

'It's nominated for all the prizes, a firm favourite for at least three of them.' His blunt finger stabs at the ornately illustrated front page. 'The blurb is written by the Pope himself.'

I sigh. Papal approval. Those prizes are nailed on then, the bloody sycophants. There's no accounting for taste. And self-published as well! It'll be the death of the industry, mark my words. The only thing worse would be if someone managed to automate the printing process, doing away with my silent scribes and lowering the bar to what it is economical and fitting to publish. God preserve us if that happens.

As Alfredo backs out of the door, I reach into my desk for the pages the now famous Dante Alighieri spilled on my floor those many months ago, Cantos 38 and 39: the Tenth Circle of Hell, trying to work out what, if anything, I'd missed in my oh-so-casual skim.

Moments later I can feel the prickly heat of a blush and am glad I am alone. I can hardly believe I was so supportive, that I spent so much of my precious time with him. And for this: to have a whole circle of hell dedicated to Booksellers, Editors, and Agents, with – of course! – the worst of the punishments expressly reserved for the Publishers.

I roll up the sheets and stuff them into the folds of my cloak. These, I think with a grimace, as I head down the steps to the cloister and the privy beyond, I will keep for my own personal use.

When Nature Calls

Gareth E. Rees

Maleeka opened the back door of their bungalow to discover that their water butt had vanished. The vegetable patch was still there. The electricity generator and greenhouse, too – just about – but where the butt had been was now thin air. Carefully she got on her knees and crawled to the cliff edge. On the shore, thirty metres below, the big green container poked from a pile of rubble, topped with bits of lawn. It was getting dark. Dirty clouds amassed over an English Channel that was rising quickly, drowning rocks and turning the sandstone blood red. Tonight's full moon meant the tide would be extra high. After a week of heavy rain, who knew what else they might lose before the morning?

She returned to the kitchen to tell Rizzie. At the news Rizzie suddenly looked much older than her sixty-seven years. 'Have we any water bottles left?'

'I filled one earlier,' said Maleeka.

'Then we can have a cuppa, at least.' Rizzie opened the cupboard above the kettle and stared into it for a while. Finally, she said, 'Where's the tea?'

'I think we finished it.'

Rizzie sighed. 'Then there's nothing to be done. Nothing.'

'You should have said.'

'It's always me, ain't it? I should have said, I should have said. What about you? What should you have said? You always wait till the last moment, right until the point when things run out. Then suddenly you pipe up. You're a late piper, that's what you are.'

'That's not true.'

'When I think of all these years you've been living here…'

There was a knock at the door.

'Shit on a stick, this is all we need,' said Rizzie, hobbling arthritically into the living room. 'If that's Brian – and I can't think who else it could possibly be – then let's kill him and steal his tea. We've sod-all to lose.'

Rizzie's parents named her Elizabeth, which she hated, but rarely heard it said from their lips. Her mum was an addict who bed-hopped through the backstreets of Brighton while dad was nothing more than a series of letters sent from oil rigs where he worked before he started a new family somewhere in Scotland. She was brought up in Hastings by Granny Stamford, or Peg as she insisted on being called. Peg was a fiercely funny armchair raconteur surrounded by books on almost every subject, from mechanical engineering and black magic to medieval poetry and archaeology. She told Rizzie that 13,000 years ago, long before the pyramids, there was a matriarchal moon-worshipping civilisation with an intricate knowledge of the stars, electricity and engineering. It thrived until a comet hit the earth, melting the North American ice sheet and causing a great flood that destroyed almost every trace of that civilisation. Men had since thrived on our amnesia.

Peg's feminist histories pleased Rizzie as a goth teenager in late '80s, skinning up for the skinny lads beneath the pier, which is how she earned her nickname. As soon as she was able, she left for London to seek emancipation. By 1993 she lived in a Leyton squat, protesting the M11 link road, a monstrous tarmac river spilling through the middle of an East London community, demolishing everything in its path. Claremont Road was the last bastion of defence, a Victorian street blocking the capitalist highway. They offered tenants cash incentives for abandoning their properties. Then they sent in bailiffs, riot cops and dogs to force out the rest. She lived for months under siege, behind boarded doors, sun slanting through the gaps, listening to protestors and police bark at each other through megaphones. The pigs won of course, as they always did. The walls torn away even as they huddled within. Houses pulled down, the new road built, and cars whizzing through the ghost of a community as if nothing had happened.

Things were never the same after that. Rizzie endured a succession of clerical office jobs that paid for enough cider at the weekend to stay hungover from Monday to Friday, when she could do it all over again. A decade passed like this before she returned to Hastings where she tried to avoid her youthful haunts and bad penny lovers who turned up on her doorstep. Fortunately, her dad died just after her thirty-sixth birthday and left her nineteen grand in his will. Guilt money, she presumed. It was enough to get a bungalow in Fairlight a few streets back from the cliff edge where she could see the sea from the garden if she stood on a bucket and peered through a gap in the houses on Sea Road. On the first day, a stray cat wandered into the house and curled up on the rug. In that instant Rizzie knew she would never call another place home.

That was almost thirty years and god knows how many cats ago. Rizzie was now the age Granny Stamford was when she died. Sea Road had since dropped into the sea, leaving her bungalow with a front row seat. She could open the door and look out over the English Channel with its storm clouds and container ships and see the helicopters buzz to Dungeness or industrial rescue vessels pump showers of rock onto the shingle around the troubled power station. Some days, hot sun beat on her greenhouse full of organic vegetables and marihuana plants. But more often, monsoon rains nourished her potatoes and leeks. On balmy evenings, she sat with her cats, listening to the hum of the generator, blowing smoke rings and drinking tea, a pleasure now lost because half her garden was at the bottom of the cliff along with a week's worth of collected rain water, and the bloody Syrian had forgotten to get tea bags.

To make things worse, here was Brian on the doorstep. Busybody twat-in-a-mac Brian with a bundle of papers in his hands. Behind him the first dots of rain fell on cracked pavements broken by buddleia and thistle. He didn't wait for Rizzie's invitation and shuffled into the living room where Maleeka was lighting candles. Rizzie was certain that Maleeka was the sole reason he remained in Fairlight. The rest of the village had taken the compensation money and run – 'managed retreat' the government called it. Bloody sell-outs. Rizzie believed it was immoral to take money for abandoning the home she loved. She'd been through this before in Leyton in '94. They said she was a fool, but if you don't live by your principles you might as well throw yourself into the ocean anyway.

'I brought something for ya to look at.' Brian thudded the papers on the coffee table, frightening a cat from under it. 'I know you ladies have something against the internet… and TVs… and phones… so I took the liberty…'

'Ha! That's bang on,' snapped Rizzie, closing the door. 'Liberties, Brian. We all got 'em, but some people want to take 'em from us. Ain't that right Leeka?'

'Very good," said Brian. 'Thing is, see, Maleeka, I wanted to show you the latest predictions. These are the fresh from the government website… coastal management 2037… moving forward to 2047.' He held up a piece of paper with map of Fairlight on it. 'We are standing, right now, all of us, above what is going to be a bay in less than a year... a bay, do you hear? The cliff won't hold. You can't stop the water.'

'Why do you assume I think water can be stopped?' said Maleeka. 'You think I don't know about water?'

'Well, y'know...' Brian blushed and looked down at his feet. 'I'm sorry, Maleeka.'

Maleeka's two children floating face down in the Aegean beside an upturned boat. That's what all three of them saw that moment, as hard rain began to fall, hammering the roof. Rizzie had found Maleeka on the streets of Hastings a year after she made it to Britain from Syria, shivering with cold. She gave her sanctuary in Fairlight where she taught her to tend the vegetable garden, feed chickens, fix the generator, swear like a trooper, and live a life off-grid. No governments, no pesticides, no fluoride, no internet, no television and no need for men. They got everything they could want from a marriage – all the collaboration, company and bickering – without the sex and physical combat. This was what made Brian so irritating, lingering in their living room with his dyed combover and meaty odour.

'I want to help,' he said, reaching for Maleeka's hand. She didn't take it. 'You don't understand the danger. Come to my place, stay a while and we'll make a plan'. He turned to Rizzie, his smile crooked. 'Of course, I – I – I mean the both of you.'

'We have five cats,' said Rizzie. 'They'll tell us when we need to move out. They can sense danger, cats. Famous for it.'

'When you see what I printed out, you'll change your tune. Just give me a chance.' Brian pointed to the hallway. 'But first can I use yer loo?' He shambled down the hall and shut the toilet door with soft click.

'What if he's right, Rizzie?' whispered Maleeka.

'Don't start.'

'Maybe it's inevitable.'

'We got years left, years I tell ya. They're all scaremongers.'

'But when it comes…'

'If it comes.'

'Sorry, Rizzie, but I believe that what's happening is the will of-'

'Don't say it, Leeka. Don't invoke his name. He who does not exist.'

Maleeka didn't know much about what was happening to the ice caps and the weather but she had never lost her faith, despite all she had suffered. It was every good Muslim's duty to nurture the earth, and she had done so to the best of her ability. But perhaps the time had come to leave their garden. Long ago the Arabian Peninsula had been a verdant meadowland. It was narrated in a hadith that the Messenger of Allah declared 'the Hour will not begin until the land of the Arabs once again becomes meadows and rivers.' Now the rains were returning like the Prophesy said. England's suffering was not her homeland's. It might be that this was the will of Allah. Perhaps the return of the meadows would bring peace to the Middle East and she could return home from exile, taking Rizzie with her.

'You're as bad as those wizards,' said Rizzie, settling into her armchair, kicking Brian's papers onto the floor so she could rest her feet on the table.

'This is different.'

'No it ain't, you all think something better's coming and you wanna cheer it on, waving your little flags.'

Maleeka remembered the wizards well enough. Not long after Sea Road collapsed and the government announced the coastal roll-back, men in black robes and tall black hats began to appear on the shore. Sharing a joint in their deck chairs at the edge of the garden, Maleeka and Rizzie watched in amusement as the men arranged coloured stones in circles and danced around fires, flicking water from buckets. A few weeks later a different group appeared, this time men in white robes and white hats. They set up further along the shore, using a similar combination of fire, water and stone. Every so often a white robed man in a pointed hat went to the water's edge and flung forward his arms, if to hurl them at the horizon. At this, a member of the black robed group went over to remonstrate, jabbing a finger angrily at the man in the white pointed hat. The man in the white pointed hat jabbed back. At which point the black hatted man knocked the white hatted man's hat right off. A scuffle broke out, punches flying, men chasing each other up and down the foreshore, pulling each other's cowls over their heads and throwing stones. It seemed to go on for hours. The next afternoon a group of black robed men knocked at the door and explained that they were from an organisation called the O.T.O – the Ordo Templi Orientis.

'I know very well who you lot are,' Rizzie said. 'Crowley's black magic lot. My grandmother met your most famous member over in Hastings almost a century ago. He was a right cunt, apparently.'

'My apologies,' said a man with a black eye and a torn black hat under his arm. 'But Aleister Crowley was the gatekeeper of the apocalypse and finally the Aeon of Horus is upon us. Our work is urgent. I wonder if we might use your garden for a ceremony, free from disturbance by… certain undesirables.'

Rizzie's heart swelled with Granny Stamford's spirit. She couldn't stop herself. She just let fly.

'What is it about you men and the apocalypse? Does it get you hard or something? Hells bloody bells! There is no apocalypse, there's only things growing and things dying and things growing again. It's how it was before us and how it'll be after we're gone. If you ever stopped to smell the fucking flowers you'd understand. Now jog on.' She slammed the door.

After a few months, the beach became too dangerous for ceremonies, and the wizards went elsewhere. The last of Fairlight's residents packed their bags and left too. Nobody had been to their door in years. Except for Brian, of course. There was always Brian.

'What the hell is he doing in there anyway?' said Rizzie staring angrily towards the toilet. 'He's been an age.'

They sat for a while, listening to the cacophony of rain and wind. Candle flames guttered as waves crashed against the cliff. A rumble of thunder, like nothing they'd ever heard before, shook the house, smashed the glasses in their cupboards and sent trinkets flying from shelves. The women jumped from their chairs in fright. What a racket! Their frantic cats paced the room, mewing loudly. Yet still no Brian.

Tentatively, Maleeka went into the hall and called out, 'Brian? Are you alright in there, Brian?… Brian?'

No reply.

'Call him 'lover' or 'darling',' said Rizzie, 'that'll do it. He'll come leaping out. You watch. Leaping out like the pranny he is.'

Maleeka giggled. 'Brian, darling!'

Another rumble of thunder.

'Oh for pity's sake,' Rizzie hobbled past Maleeka and shook the handle, but the door was locked. She rapped on the wood. 'Open up, Brian! Open up, you swine!'

'There must be something wrong,' said Maleeka. 'I'll give it a kick.'

'You what?'

'Like this,' Maleeka raised a foot and slammed it hard into the door. It swung open to reveal a universe in collapse. A mass of sulphurous cloud swirled towards the moon in a roar of noise, as if the world was being sucked through a vent in space. The English Channel was a seething tumult, the waves an infinity of shark fins racing inland. With a cry, they held onto each other tight, bracing themselves in the doorway to oblivion. At their feet was a sheer drop to a sea fizzing with acid rain. The entire back wall and floor of the toilet were gone. Only the side walls remained, jutting out over the cliff. The toilet roll, still in its holder, was unspooled all the way down, a ribbon of white paper dangling into the blackness like the world's worst bungee cord. Brian was about to wipe when the floor gave way, and held on to the paper until the very end. Below them, water exploded against rock. Chunks of wood and plaster spun in phosphorescent foam. But no sign of Brian. He was gone.

'Well that's the end of that,' muttered Rizzie. She felt nothing but a hole where her heart had been.

'Brian!' Maleeka cried into the rain. 'Brian, I'm sorry!' Twenty years fell away and an ocean of pain rushed in. 'My children, my children, my children...'

For a moment, they stared into the sea which had taken their generator, their greenhouse, their toilet, their neighbour, and turned them to flotsam. Then they fled to the living room, where their terrified cats scratched at the porch door. They grabbed their coats. There was no need for keys. Not anymore. It was time to run. Rizzie knew that now. You can ignore the prophets, the politicians and all the Brians. But when nature calls, everyone must listen.

The Best Way
to Kill a Butterfly

Hannah Stevens

For reasons nobody seemed sure of, butterflies filled the skies like flocks of birds that summer. Young children stood on streets with arms extended, their sleeves covered with fluttering wings. National newspapers ran the story on their front pages and footage was played over and over on television screens. Temperatures were the hottest on record but Tess wore black and let her skin burn. It was the summer Madeline would've been born.

The street where Tess lived was wide and leafy and in the front garden there was a buddleia bush she didn't cut back anymore. In the cooler spring she'd noticed how the dark leaves had been eaten away to heart shaped skeletons. The chrysalis of hundreds of caterpillars had hung from the green spines of the leaves. It was a surprise to see the branches foam with purple flowers when summer came. Across the road there was a park and people with pushchairs and cameras came to visit the expanse of well-tended flowerbeds. They'd disappear a few hours later with blistered skin and photographs of bright blossoms on bare, leafless stalks.

Every day that summer, Tess got home to find butterflies fluttering against the opaque panes of the bathroom window. She wondered how they could be so blind and why, after so many attempts at the same piece of glass, they didn't look for another way out. The first time it happened she was home late. Work was busy and she didn't rush to get back to an empty house. Walking into the bathroom she saw the butterfly's silhouette, dark against the sun that still shone through the glass. There were lilac eyes on its wings. The fur on its body shivered in a slight breeze. She fetched a mug from the kitchen cupboard and picked up an envelope from the sideboard.

Then she stepped onto the edge of the bath and leant forward to place the mug over its body. The plastic ledge was still wet from her shower that morning and her bare feet began to slip. She fell forward then and the mug hit the window. As her temple hit the tap of the bath she heard the ceramic smash on the floor. The butterfly landed silently on the tiles.

Michael had left days ago and so nobody came to see what the noise was or if she was okay.

It was a few minutes before Tess sat up. The butterfly's antennae still twitched: its torn-away wing lay on the windowsill. Tess picked up a flat shard of the broken mug and pressed it quickly over its body. There was a noise like the crumpling of paper.

After that, Tess kept the windows closed. She checked them twice and turned the latch to *locked* whenever she left the house. But every day she came home to the faint noise of wings fluttering against glass. She would catch them in her hands now and their wings felt like feathers in her palms. She would take them outside and throw them towards the sky, like she had hands full of confetti, then she would wait for a second and hope they'd fly away. Most of the time they didn't, but still she did this and hoped.

Soon there were stories about a new craze. Every newspaper reported it on their front page and people talked of it wherever you went. The butterflies could be pressed between glass and mounted in frames you could hang in your hallways. They could be trapped in pendants made with silver and varnish and threaded onto chains you wore around your neck. Small ones could be fashioned into rings for your fingers. Why wouldn't you want your own piece of this pretty phenomenon? There were enough of them to go around, after all. The how-to books said the killing method was simple. You did it like this:

The best way to kill a butterfly is to pinch its thorax between your thumb and forefinger. The thorax is the middle segment of the butterfly's body and is the fattest part of the insect. You must learn the correct pressure and this technique takes practice. It will stun the specimen and prevent it from damaging itself. The specimen can then be slipped into an envelope or a tight-fitting box with insecticide and kept indefinitely until mounted or made into jewellery.

For those who want to add caterpillars to their collection it is advisable to drown them in a preservative fluid or to boil them like shrimp.

At dinner parties it became customary to have butterfly centrepieces. The insects would be pinned to cork and cased behind beautiful frames. After eating, guests were given nets and jars and there were competitions over who could catch the one considered the prettiest. Those who took part chose between Red Admirals, purple-eyed Peacocks and Orange Monarchs with wings like stained glass windows. Cabbage Whites were mostly left alone or given to children as tiny trophies for good behaviour. Winners got to keep their butterfly and were issued with pins and boards to make their own souvenir when they got home. Runners-up left their dead butterflies on sideboards or patio slabs to be swept and tidied away the next day.

Tess was going to be late for dinner. She'd got away from work on time but the heat was heavy and thick and it made her move slowly. Upstairs she'd opened the sash window and sat on her bed. The blankets were warm from the sunshine and she took off her clothes. Outside there was the noise from the road. She could hear the wheels of pushchairs and people talking and she could see the features of their faces. There were curtains at the sash but she didn't close them. She knew that if they looked up towards her window they would see her and she wondered what they would think if they did. She would shower soon and get ready to go out. But first she would lie down for a few minutes and maybe she would fall asleep. It didn't matter that she would arrive late because she knew that everyone would say, *it's okay Tess, we understand.* The sun shone through the window and fell across her shoulders. She closed her eyes and in a few minutes her skin began to burn.

When she woke, her shoulders were sore. She turned her head and saw the red mark across her skin. She stood and stretched. Her scalp felt tight and she could feel the heat from the sun beneath her hair: the back of her head was burnt too. Outside she saw Drew from next door. He was back from work and he locked his car. Tess stepped towards the window and he turned towards the house. She watched him look up but she didn't move. She knew that he could see her.

'You're so late,' said Tess's friend when she opened the front door, 'I didn't think you were coming.'

'I fell asleep when I got home from work,' said Tess, 'and look: I got burnt from lying in the sun.' Tess turned away then to show her the red patches across her shoulder blades. As she turned, her friend placed her palm onto the green wood of the door. Tess heard it click into place as it closed and she saw a ring on her hand.

'What do you think?' she said. The black and blue butterfly wing was cased in clear resin and mounted on silver. 'I found it in the garden - didn't even have to go to the park for the buddleia bushes. I pinned the butterfly to the board and took off the wing myself,' she said.

There was bottle of white wine in Tess's hand and the glass felt cold and slippery in her fingers. She wondered if the butterflies bled when people put pins in them and, even if they did, did anyone notice. 'I took the wing to the jeweller on the same day because I already knew what I wanted. She said it was a really neat cut when I got there. Nothing torn or frayed and it was perfectly intact. Isn't it beautiful?'

'It's not really my taste,' said Tess. Her friend was silent and for a second she looked at her as if she didn't understand. The bottle began to slip from Tess's hand but she didn't tighten her grip. She felt it slide from her grasp and the glass smashed when it hit the coloured tiles of the floor. She noticed the shards on the ground, and how some were small enough to pick up and place inside her mouth. She bent down and put a piece in her palm.

'Fuck,' said Tess's friend, 'don't move. Your sandals are so thin you'll get something stuck in your foot. Wait here while I get a brush. Don't worry, we all know it's been a difficult time for you.'

Tess could hear voices from the back rooms.

'When are we catching these butterflies?' someone said. 'And does the winner get a bottle of wine too?' There was the sound of laughing. Tess opened the front door and stepped quietly onto the street.

After it happened it was as if Michael had got up and left. It was as if they both had except they were still there. When they ate it was like they weren't really eating at all, because food tasted of nothing and it was difficult to swallow. And when they fucked, it was like they weren't really fucking at all. They would twist and kneel in their usual positions and sometimes they made a noise so they could pretend they were having fun. But what they were really thinking about was how long it would be before they could go to sleep.

Tess hadn't seen Michael cry since it had happened. Or get angry. She wondered if he blamed her and she hoped that he did because she wanted to be blamed.

The bedroom window was open and in the heat and the darkness there was the smell of blossom. They were in bed and fucking and in the dark she couldn't make out his face. She looked down and traced the silhouette of his head against the pillows. He was quiet aside from his breathing which was only a little faster than when he was beginning to fall asleep. *He's barely here*, she'd thought and then she'd wanted to hurt him. She'd moved quickly, bending her knees, kneeling on his chest and pressing down with all her weight. He'd said something she couldn't make out and then she'd bitten his lip hard between her teeth. He inhaled sharply and she pushed down harder so the air rushed from his mouth. For a few seconds they didn't move.

There was no air in his lungs and her weight pressed him to the bed. He felt his heart begin to beat faster. Blood rushed in his ears and his lip throbbed. It was still in her mouth and he felt her breath on his face. His eyes were open wide and the darkness was pricked with purple and blue. He began to panic then and pushed her. He felt the flatness of her stomach beneath his hand and the gaps between her ribs.

There was a thud when she fell to the floor, but otherwise she didn't make a sound. At the window he saw moths fluttering at the glass of the raised sash. There was a streetlight outside and they tried to get to it. Michael felt sick and the heat of the room made it hard for him to catch his breath. Tess stood and moved to the arch of the door. He noticed that she walked slowly and held her arm but he didn't ask where it hurt or if she was okay.

In the bathroom she switched on the light. She turned towards the mirror and saw that there was a bruise coming. She'd landed on her shoulder and it felt full of knots and aches. She imagined that there would be patches of purple and blue down to her elbow soon and she thought that it felt good to feel hurt in some other way. She'd waited in the doorway for him to say something: for him to call her a fucking bitch and ask what she thought she was doing, but he hadn't. He'd stayed silent on the bed and so she'd walked away. She'd slept on the settee for the rest of the night. The leather cushions felt cool beneath her and when she woke up she'd felt cold and she'd shivered.

Michael heard her close the bathroom door and walk downstairs. He switched on the light and looked for his bag. He chose
a pair of shoes from the bottom of the wardrobe and covered
them with trousers, shorts, some shirts, a hat. He laughed: it
was like packing for a holiday, except he wasn't. Tomorrow he'd
catch the train and get off at the coast. It didn't matter which
one so he'd choose the one with the cheapest fare. When he
leaves she'll be glad, because the silences won't be heavy and
tense and at night she can go to sleep with the light on.

At the coast Michael had expected fewer butterflies. But there
were fields and flowers and trees close to the sea and so the
butterflies filled the sky like at home. He saw gulls at the beach
swoop and swallow them in their beaks. There were lots of fam-
ilies on holiday and he guessed it was the heat that had brought
them all here. The sun burned in the sky and he was glad he was
wearing his hat. Children were building sandcastles and eating
sandwiches. People were paddling and taking photographs. He
stepped onto the sand and it felt hot beneath his bare feet. As
he neared the sea he noticed that tangled in the seaweed and
the shale were the faded, broken wings of butterflies. He bent
down and picked one up. It turned to powder in his fingertips
and left sharp grains of sand in his hands.
The water is cold in spite of the sun and his feet ache as he
steps under the waves. As he walks, he turns to see the beach
behind him. The wind blows in the wrong direction for him

to hear but he sees a child crying. The child's mother is trying to swot away butterflies that crowd around the sticky, white ice cream he has in his hands. The butterflies launch and dart towards the cone and he has never seen them move like that before. He wonders what they usually eat and if it is the sugar or the coolness that they like in the scorching heat. The mother waves her hands and he thinks of dancing and of being drunk. The child drops the ice cream and then he watches as the mother stamps on the mush of white and sand and butterflies. Michael turns away and traces the line on the horizon where the sea meets the sky.

Later, at the B&B, Michael isn't alone. It's a cheap room. The curtains are heavy and old and the carpet doesn't match. It had still been light when he'd checked in and he'd saw dust caught in the shards of light that fell through the gaps in the closed curtains. Even though he'd guessed they'd been drawn to stop the furniture from fading, he'd opened them anyway. There was no view of the sea from here: most of the other rooms were taken and when he'd checked in they didn't think he looked like the kind of man who would care.

Michael is on his knees and fucking a woman he doesn't love from behind. They are on a four-poster bed and he thinks that it's out of place. There is a circus in town and they met there earlier. He thought of the flashing lights, the drum rolls and the cold beer he drank straight from the can. He thought of the rose he caught, thrown in to the crowd during one of the shows, and how he offered it to her because he didn't know what to do with it.

'You really shouldn't have,' she said and then she'd laughed.

'What's your name?' he said.

'Adel,' she said.

'Do you work here?' he said and he gestured towards the tents and the lights and the crowd.

'Kind of,' she said, 'but mostly I'm just sleeping with one of the clowns.'

When they'd finished fucking she smiled.

'I ran away from home and my husband to be with a circus clown,' she said, and then she laughs. Michael lies down on the bed and pulls the sheet over his chest. He doesn't know this woman and he hasn't done this for a long time. He doesn't know if he should hold her and he isn't sure that he wants to. She begins to get dressed.

'The clown is a woman, you know. But sometimes...,' she pauses, 'I wonder that I might miss this.' She gestures towards him and then pulls her t-shirt over her head. 'But I've decided that I don't, in case you wondered. It's just, I needed to feel sure. And now I know, so thank you.' He doesn't know what he should say to this but it's OK because now she's kissing him. Her tongue is in his mouth and it tastes sweet and then she says goodbye and closes the door behind her.

By mid-September torn wings and mashed bodies of butterflies blew through the streets. The newly dead squelched and slipped underfoot while older ones rustled and crunched like dead leaves. Tess was in the garden hanging out sheets that smelt of lime. There were voices and she looked across the low fence. It was Tom and his dad, Drew. She wondered how old Tom was and guessed that it was somewhere around five. She watched as Tom's father took a butterfly from the net in his hand and slowly squeezed its middle. There was a pop as its abdomen burst and she watched as its black body turned to a sticky mess between his fingers. Tom squealed and it reminded Tess of the slaughterhouse noises her father had told her about.

'Don't worry, son, we'll soon catch another one,' Tom's father said as he wiped the black smudge onto his jeans. Tess noticed Drew's hands and how they were tanned. She wondered how his fingers would feel in her mouth and then she stepped closer to the fence.

She watched as the boy walked back inside. His face was pink and hot and she knew that he was about to cry.

'Hello,' she said, 'how's the butterfly catching going?' Drew turned around.

'Hello,' he said, 'not that great actually. Well, the catching is okay – they're slow and stupid because of the heat. And obviously there are so many of them that they'd be difficult to miss. It's just, I keep squashing them.' He checked his thumb and pulled a face at the dark stain on his fingers. 'We've never spoken before have we,' he said and she knew this wasn't really a question.

'No, she said, 'though I've seen you from my window.' She watched him blush. 'It's been a strange time. I'm sorry I haven't introduced myself. Welcome to the street.' She laughed then and made a gesture with her arm. He smiled and dropped the net he'd been holding to the floor.

'Thanks,' he said, 'and yes, these are strange times.' He pointed to the butterflies that had landed on his chest. Tess counted six of them and then nodded although that wasn't what she meant.

There were birds on the grass: a female chaffinch and her orange mate. They were fat because of the good summer and Tess saw butterflies crumpling in their beaks as they ate them.

'I'm here alone at the moment,' she said. 'Michael has left and I don't know if he's coming back.'

'Oh,' said Drew, 'I'm sorry,' and he noticed that there was a ring with a diamond on her left hand.

'Are you free later?' she said. He looked at her then, right in her eyes, and he understood that she was offering him something.

'I can come over for eight,' he said, and he didn't even pause before he said this.

'I'll leave the door unlocked,' she said and then she turned and finished hanging the sheets on the line.

It's cooler in the house and Drew is glad. He watches her from the window in the kitchen. It doesn't take her long to string the washing from the cord that stretches across the garden. She's hanging bed sheets and pillow cases and they are all black. He has never laid on black sheets before and he wonders if tonight he will. Abby is in the living room and he can hear that the television is on. Tom has stopped crying over the crushed butterfly. Drew wonders what he will tell them when he leaves to go next door, when he leaves to do something he will never want them to know about.

It was still light when Tess heard the door being pushed open from the outside. She swallowed the last of the wine in her glass and put it onto the coffee table.

'Hello,' he said. His voice was quiet and it shook at the edges. She stood and walked across the carpet with bare feet. She knew he wouldn't be able to hear her yet because she was too far away. He hadn't moved since he closed the door and she knew that the hallway would seem dim now he was inside. She wondered what her house would smell like to him and if he looked up the stairs and to the landing and wondered if that was where he should wait. She wanted to get to him before he spoke again: she thought it would be better if they didn't talk. She stood in the doorway and he saw her. She put her finger across her closed lips and Drew understood what this meant. His hands shook as he placed them around her waist and he wondered if she noticed.

Later when Drew goes home there's a scratch that traces from his shoulder blade down to his thigh. He knows that it's there but he doesn't see it until the next day when he's in the bathroom with the door locked. He wonders how long it will take to fade. It was dark when he got home and the house was quiet and still. Abby was asleep in their bed and she felt warm when he slid in beside her. Usually he slept naked when it was hot, but tonight he wore his t-shirt and felt glad that Tess didn't wear perfume.

That morning Michael called Tess and asked if he could come home. His voice was quiet and broken on the phone and he was sorry. He'd called her from a pay phone because he'd lost his mobile and can you believe they even still exist he'd asked.

'It's lucky that they do,' she said.

'And what about all the butterflies?' he said. 'There's still so many of them, even now.'

'I know,' said Tess. 'And isn't it sad what people are doing to them?'

She hadn't blamed him for leaving. It'd been difficult to find the words afterwards. What did people expect? Michael had woken to screams in the night as Tess almost bled to death on the sheets of their bed. A few minutes later there had been something small like a doll that, for a minute or two, had felt warm when Michael had held her. They'd called her Madeline and she was buried in a coffin Michael had carried in one of his hands. Nothing was going to be okay after that.

Madeline's room was mostly empty now. The pile of the car-

pet was deep and warm under Tess's feet and there was a ted-
dy bear that wore a silk ribbon. As she'd stepped through the
door, Tess had heard the noise of wings beating against glass.
She'd stepped forward as the butterfly landed and she watched
as it tapped quickly across the panes. Michael was coming
home today. He'd asked her if he could and she'd said yes,
that she wanted him here. The summer was beginning to fade
away and wasn't autumn their favourite time. Tess unlocked
the heavy brass catch of the frame and pushed open the window. The breeze was cooler than it had been for months and
she felt the hairs rise on her arms. She stood then, with her
palm on the cold wall and she watched as the pale Cabbage
White fluttered out into the wide, silver sky.

Confessions of an Irresolute Ethnic Writer

Elaine Chiew

'He who is willing to work gives birth to his own father.' – Kierkegaard

The Ethnic Writer was a somnambulist, also a whiner. He should be writing, but spent many hours thinking about consistent narrative voice, and examining every zit on his countenance or simply gazing at his own visage in the mirror and making faces. The Yellow Peril Face. The Fu Manchu Face. The Charlie Chan Face. The Fresh-Off-The-Boat Face. The Model Minority Eager Beaver Face. Which one was his True Face?

When he couldn't sleep at night, he would pad around his apartment in flip-flops and eat Maltesers. He was garrulous, accustomed to pulling his lower lip in a rant of one kind or another. He was a doodler of Disney characters. Goofy was his best imitation. When he couldn't write, he blasted Bruce Springsteen very loudly and used his wireless mouse as a microphone in off-pitch karaoke renditions. His invocations for his muse were alliterative jingles – *moose for a goose, how about it? Shitty Chinamen in cities shine your shoes.*

Garuda[1] arrived early this morning, swooping down onto the windowsill like a dark angel, the turtle and the elephant in his talons tired of squirming, lying limpid with staring eyes like victims. Garuda had been watching the Ethnic Writer since this morning. The young man didn't look very chewable or appetising. He ranted about political fiction and the limitations of fictional frameworks and this made Garuda think he might taste leathery. Although the Ethnic Writer was not bad-looking – full head of black hair, nice sloe eyes (the Ethnic Writer was having an internal wrangle over whether to use that description, even if in ironic jest), Garuda suspected he might be bony and full of cartilage given his sparrow ribcage and muscly thighs. Was the Ethnic Writer possibly a Brahman? Must not on any account eat one of those.

It felt like yesterday still to Garuda, in a timeless out-of-time kind of way – his encounter with his father Kasyapa. Wasn't it just like fathers to be prescriptive without being helpful? Kasyapa had told him to seek out the elephant and turtle quarrelling in the lake and to go eat them on Rauhina, the Tree that could Speak. Kasyapa hadn't provided directions or sonar navigational tips – how was he expected to locate Rauhina, this old friend of his father's? Garuda billowed out his wings and launched himself into the skies. He flew thou-

---

1 A large, mythical bird-like creature in Buddhist and Hindu mythology.

sands of leagues. It was all very tiresome, because the skies were leaden, filled with sulphurous, dense clouds. Periodically, he flew through ionic patches and got zapped. Then without warning he must have flown into the eye of turbulence – he felt weightless without any sensation of his extremities and then, that drop of vertigo, *oh what a rush*, like that infamous girl in literature with the pinafore and that rabbit tunnel! Darkness all around, with the occasional twinkle of lights in outer perimeters. Wind tore at him, lashed him and spun him about. He fell out of the sky and his bottom hit a slushy element, something moist and soft. Gazing down, he realised what it was. People who own dogs should be more responsible.

Where was he? The elephant and turtle had both got bonked on their heads in that crash landing and were swooning. Then, Garuda saw this lighted window – some kind of schmaltzy apartment complex where the inhabitants dumped their garbage in Tesco plastic bags to be later scavenged by errant foxes and mongrel dogs. It was so early in the morning that everything was swathed in semi-darkness, all except this window with its blazing square of yellow light. Here he'd been, until the Ethnic Writer roused from his onanistic reverie and deigned to notice him.

Upon noticing the outsized shadow grazing his wall, the Ethnic Writer emitted a short yelp, then said with great tone control, 'Em…who or what are you? What are you doing on my windowsill?'

Garuda shook his blue-black wings and folded them. His

claws gently pushed elephant and turtle over to one side. 'Ka,' he said.

'Ha?' the Ethnic Writer said.

'No, Ka.'

'What?' the Ethnic Writer sneaked a look at his own face in the mirror, and the wide panic in his eyes made him self-conscious.

'I'm hungry and looking for something to eat,' Garuda said.

This seemed to scare the Ethnic Writer out of his wits. 'Are those an elephant and a turtle you have there?'

Garuda shook his feathers. 'They are whatever you think they are.'

The Ethnic Writer shook his head as if to clear it. 'All I have are Weetabix and Greek yoghurt. If you want I can rustle up an egg. But the pan is gunked up with charred stuff and I'd rather not have to wash it.'

Garuda frowned. 'Have you a tree anywhere on the vicinity?'

The Ethnic Writer shrugged. He was used to non-sequiturs, being a writer. 'I have a ficus that's dying in the kitchen. Will that do?'

They repaired to the kitchen where the Ethnic Writer got out two melamine bowls and cups. 'Coffee?'

Garuda examined the ficus. It was dry and crackly and the minute one of his claws touched a branch, it snapped off, which filled Garuda with foreboding. The Ethnic Writer poured milk on his Weetabix, shoved in a mouthful and started grinding his molars. The sounds he produced were so much like the crunching of bones that Garuda looked at him with new respect. Perhaps the Ethnic Writer was very lonely, perhaps he'd been too marginalised, or perhaps he was exercising his imaginative capabilities, because he didn't think there was anything odd about having a half-man half-eagle sitting in his kitchen, clutching an elephant and a turtle that were Lilliputian. Or perhaps he was possessed of great presence of mind by virtue of being wily and manipulative and having to dance on his toes around the perimeters of exclusion/ non-exclusion.

As if to demonstrate this particular virtue, the Ethnic Writer asked conversationally, 'What brings you to town, or specifically, to my window?'

'Where am I?' said Garuda.

'Birmingham. West Midlands.'

'But you're not from Birmingham. Where are you really from?'

The Ethnic Writer became visibly agitated at this question. 'Does it matter so much? I'm here now.'

This meant nothing to Garuda. So he told the Ethnic Writer about his mission to bring *soma* to liberate his mother from slavery.

'What's soma?' the Ethnic Writer asked.

Garuda was shocked. 'You don't seem to know your mythology.'

The Ethnic Writer blanched. 'Don't tell me what I know or don't know.'

Garuda nodded sagely. 'You know Beowulf? Odin? This is

a drink that marked the passage from nature to culture. You know it as mead.'

'Of course I know mead,' the Ethnic Writer said tersely.

Garuda told about being hatched from an egg and about his beautiful mother Vinatā. The curse of his brother Aruna, the Suryā's charioteer, on his mother. She'd been too impatient waiting for Aruna to hatch and broke his shell before it was time. He'd emerged only half-formed, and angry at being given only a half-measure of existence, he sentenced her to be her sister's slave for five hundred years. The Ethnic Writer listened avidly, drew a breath and experienced a mini-epiphany. 'My god! How did I not see it before? You're a hallucination of my mind. Sent here to help me find my destiny. You're my reflection in mythology – here to help me excavate the fantasy of living, the quantum disreality of it. Like a short story. It's fiction, except peel away the layers, at the core you will find your own truth.'

Garuda was puzzled by the Ethnic Writer's obsessive mulling of his writerly existence. Nevertheless, Garuda talked about his search for his father and wanting to know more than the circumstances of his birth. As he talked, Garuda felt pain and anguish and desire build within him, reaching such a high-water mark that a wracked caw broke out from his curved beak and rattled the windowpanes. This awed the Ethnic Writer whose mocha brown eyes became wide and round with wonder and mystery. 'I see. I see it now. Love, honour, pride, pity, compassion, sacrifice. It all comes back to the father.' He gave a self-deprecating laugh and flicked his boyish hair back. 'Which in this case, being a writer, for me it's Faulkner!'

Garuda shivered. The Ethnic Writer's apartment was cold. Again, he wondered if the Ethnic Writer could possibly be a Brahman. He stretched his wings. The dark violet curtain of it rose up like a shroud. The Ethnic Writer sighed. 'What must it be like to be you? To be able to fly so high and look down on us mere mortals?'

The Ethnic Writer had a lot to say. His father had wanted him to be a lawyer. Or an engineer. Or a doctor. Never on any account one of these amorphous, ambiguous titles with no discernible boundaries and no upward mobility. He had defied his father's wishes because he didn't believe any of those professions his father wanted and so against his natural inclinations would help him contribute something substantial to mankind. He was filled with delusions of grandeur. Yet, he was strangely diffident. He was full of doubt as to his talent and misgivings as to his calling. He didn't want to be pigeonholed as an Ethnic Writer.

The Ethnic Writer debated himself as to whether or not he really had a true voice. He talked about his stories: stories filled with flights of fancy, as far as his imagination could carry him – a white woman on vacation and meeting a noodle collector; two chefs trying to teach young juvenile delinquents how to cook; a Japanese woman on the edge of adultery just because of the way a knife is handled. Perhaps he was proving something to himself. That he could write beyond what he knew. The voice of a woman, no less. The voice of a white woman, no less. When he wrote these stories, he felt he became all those characters. He knew their faces like his own. Though they felt true, still he felt as if he wrote them to avoid the understory: the one he now yearned to tell, except the contours kept eluding him.

Garuda looked at the muscle ticking in the Ethnic Writer's cheek – it beat like an avaricious pulse – and he wondered if the Ethnic Writer with his power over words and syllables could help him steal the soma for his mother. There was so much Garuda wanted to know. Who was his father? How was he conceived? Why couldn't he eat a Brahman? But even the few times that he'd located his father deep in a medieval forest, Garuda had felt tongue-tied, unable to make his mouth form the words that contained the meanings of what he sought. What deep irony from he who was himself composed of syllables – *gayatri*, *tristubh* and *jagati*.

'The solution must be in words. In language.' The Ethnic Writer's eyes had turned defiant. 'I used to know this. Oranges aren't the only fruit. The power of words is in the word itself. Something like that.'

'I don't mean to be rude and interrupt you,' Garuda said, thinking *perhaps I won't eat you after all*, 'but I really must get on. I've got some things to do.'

The Ethnic Writer looked at once earnest and disconsolate.

'The question is no longer what one talks about when one talks about race. But rather, what more can one talk about when one talks about race? Hasn't everything that needed to be said already been said?'

What was the point of this one-sided conversation? Garuda took pity on him. 'Perhaps you might like to come along?' Garuda asked. 'I promise I won't eat you if you help me find soma.'

The Ethnic Writer rushed to put on his Birkenstocks and retrieve his satchel with Dictaphone and notebook. How often he'd wanted to travel beyond himself, to escape the confines of his own skin. Now was his chance. He clambered up on top of Garuda's shoulders, and really, he'd never imagined that the triangular scapulas riding each side of Garuda would feel so much like camel-humps. 'I might die doing this,' he screamed against the gales of wind as they coasted up and up on pockets of air currents. 'But probably it will be the most meaningful thing I've ever done in my life.'

Garuda enjoyed listening to this tortured soul as he produced a stream of words that reflected an inner perverse logic. The Ethnic Writer was introspective in a way that Garuda felt himself to be when he was in flight.

It wasn't long before they flew beyond the perimeters of city blocks and electrical power-lines. The roads snaked and crossed in cloverleaf patterns. Patches of floret-like greenery interspersed with wide open fields and rolled hay and blue hills. The Ethnic Writer waved his hand about as if he was riding bronco. 'Can you understand my crossroad? If I write only of myself, it might reduce my life to its skimpy minority nature. I am that ethnic writer who fears that gradually, this reduction or deminimisation will reduce me in the end to my race. But will I be true if I write beyond myself? Will I only succeed in deceiving myself?'

They were flying over golden wheat fields, now and then dotted with farm machinery crawling slowly like individual black ants against counterpanes of yellow. On the top of a brown low-slung hill stood a lone tree, tubular, spreading its shade along the ground with its leafy branches. Garuda's stomach growled. 'Mind if I make a pit stop?' He swooped down low. The dip downwards quite took the Ethnic Writer's breath away.

They landed in a field where bales of hay rolled up here and there looked like giant curlers on blond hair. A red-roof barn tilted in the far distance. Garuda flew up and alighted on a branch. He was famished. The elephant and turtle cast their surrendering eyes at him, and he opened his beak, revealing a great maw of darkness, fathoms-deep. But despite their sacrificial expressions, Garuda felt an instinct bubbling within him – that it was wrong to eat them now. There was a time and place. With a rumbling hiss that seemed to emanate from the acids in his stomach, Garuda sucked the air, and the worms, squirrels, bugs, beetles and other creepy-crawly inhabitants in the trunk of the tree were vacuumed up into this black cavity and extinguished.

The Ethnic Writer stopped talking mid-track. 'Did I just see what I just saw? Holy schmoly, how'd you do that?'

Sadly, Garuda was still hungry. He looked around for something else to eat. The leaves of this particular tree – an oak or something – looked dusty and twiggy, and he remembered the thousand coiling black snakes around Kadru, his mother's sister. Those coiling black snakes were his half-brothers, but damn, they looked plenty savoury. He looked at the Ethnic Writer and was tempted. The Ethnic Writer started babbling.

Put-putting up a dusty road-track fenced on both sides with stiles was a farmer in his tractor. Garuda immediately inclined his head that way. He eyed the farmer. He eyed the tractor. The Ethnic Writer took a comb out of his satchel and began to toy with it like a 1970s movie star in extreme nervousness.

Garuda lifted his wings. To see him launch himself airborne was a magnificent sight – the giant brush and collaring of his wings, his legs curled up underneath, the swift descent, the sudden darkening, the farmer's turned-up face frozen in fright, the fraction-of-a-second disappearance of farmer and tractor, scooped up like a ball of ice-cream.

Now sated, they took off again, passing fields, stiles, hay bales, sheep, sheep and cow, brown-roofed barns and brown-roofed houses. The edges of a forest, like a child's irregular pencil markings. It could be a fairy tale. It was a long while before the Ethnic Writer could speak. He craned his head and looked down – the elephant and turtle had dozed off, as stiff as carcasses. 'There is nothing more peaceful or pastoral than rolling pastures and giant balls of hay,' he said, 'perhaps I am a new breed altogether – having lived in Phnom Penh, Mi-ami, Beijing, Norwich and now Birmingham, I am that Ethnic

Writer who has the diaspora all mixed within me, like salami or sausages. Not just one part of the pig, but all parts, anus and entrails included.' Garuda could but listen to this with equanimity.

They crested a hill, its summit fashioned with craggy outcrops of rock, and a sun-haze around it created a perturbation of the air, which they did not perceive until they'd flown straight into its maelstrom. It was like flying into the glow of a fire, one moment cold, the next piping hot. There was a detectable shift in the wind. Garuda's giant wings flapped once, twice, and then hovered; he'd felt a gentle sucking resistance, as if he was being palpated by a mouth and then spat out. With determination, he beat his wings, and the air-rush underneath propelled them up twisting, twisting, piercing this imperceptible membrane, and all at once, they felt that everything was different, although the scenery hadn't changed at all. Yet, the gradations of colour were more vivid somehow, the riverine glinting beneath the dappled leaves more scintillating, the blades of grass all various hues of green. *Was this what it was like when you came face to face with death?* the Ethnic Writer thought, life became more compelling, more digestible with every in-drawn rasp? The temperature had distinctly risen.

Far below, sitting beside the banks of the river was a balding man in a dhoti. He looked like a mendicant, as perhaps he was. Garuda made a beeline for this quarry.

'Please don't eat him,' the Ethnic Writer begged. 'Are you going to eat him?'

'I don't know yet,' said Garuda.

The Ethnic Writer crossed his arms and slapped his wrists with his hands. 'Please don't. He's a priest of some sort.'

Garuda shivered. A Brahman! That was one of his commandments.

'Besides, my shivery unconscious can't handle another wanton killing,' the Ethnic Writer proclaimed.

The mendicant looked up squinting as they approached. His glasses glinted in the sunlight. His wrinkly bald pate also glinted in the sunlight. His cheeks were round and doughy as dumplings. The mendicant reminded Garuda of his father, and this filled him with a pang of longing. And guilt. And foreboding.

'It's a curse that such a great one as yourself should be yoked with someone so puny,' he shouted to Garuda. His voice had a phlegmy timbre and his eyes were rheumy and vacant as if he was doped up.

The Ethnic Writer rolled his eyes.

'My son, I have a message for you. You have deviated from your one true path.' His gaze, milky and unfocussed, roved over both of them.

'Are you referring to me?' the Ethnic Writer shouted, but even so, his words were borne away willy-nilly by the moderately violent breeze.

'All you have are words. You have not carried out one jot of your mission. You have shown neither passion nor compassion.' The mendicant picked up a branch from the ground.

He swished it about, producing a whap, whap! as if against the hide of an imaginary buffalo. Garuda hung his head, ashamed. The Ethnic Writer felt his cheeks reddening with defensiveness.

'Waste no more time. You are to go north. Find ice. Find hills pockmarked with caves. You are to bring this branch. That's where you can finally dispose of that wretched elephant and turtle.'

'I need to explain to Father,' Garuda said.

The mendicant pursed his lips. 'And what good will that do?' There was no answer for this. None that would satisfy. Garuda knew this.

'If you want to have hope of penance, read the Vedas,' the mendicant advised.

'What about me?' the Ethnic Writer said.

'What about you?'

'What's to be my fate?'

'How should I know?' The mendicant turned his head towards the wind. Tufts of hair around his ears ruffled in the breeze. His dhoti curled around his legs, sinuous.

A voice spoke up. 'Is the diaspora within you?' The voice was coming from the tree, and its hollow echo sounded like it was issuing from deep within its trunk.

'Diaspora?' Having recently had thoughts along the same lines, the Ethnic Writer perked up his ears.

'Mythology is but an appropriation of metaphor. Metaphor is but an appropriation of story. Were you not born in a third world developing country?'

'Why yes.' The Ethnic Writer felt caught out, guilty.

'Child, it shouldn't matter what you write about so long as you enslave yourself to the story.'

'Ah yes,' the Ethnic Writer smiled, reminded of something. 'In my MFA program, they said that a lot.'

The elephant and turtle had woken up. One trumpeted meekly and the other waddled its legs. The Ethnic Writer felt sorry that they would die an ignominious death.

'I do so want to write good stories.' The last word ended on a falsetto, as if the Ethnic Writer were revisiting puberty.

'Well then, do so. Lose yourself. Get lost more often.'

This felt like mouse-droppings of apocrypha and he hastened to get out notepad and pencil to jot it all down. He licked his pencil and repeated each word he jotted down, '… lose yourself. Wow, that's good shit.'

'But honestly, you should stop writing.'

'What? Why?' The Ethnic Writer stopped writing. The heat of the day had left damp patches of sweat in his underarms and back, and now the stickiness began to bother him. The pad was damp underneath his fist and the words had smeared a little.

'You die infinitesimally with every story you write. It is your curse.'

This silenced the Ethnic Writer. He could not react to this or take this in.

In the north, a diffuse light was growing, and a smell of

turpentine wafted from somewhere. Garuda felt the plangent call of his mother. *Garuda.* He flexed his muscles, fluffed his feathers, stiffened his spine, sniffed the air.

'What's happening?' the Ethnic Writer stood up. He was good with trusting his instincts.

'It is time to go.' Garuda bowed to the mendicant. 'There's no time to lose.'

The Ethnic Writer wriggled his eyebrows. He was feeling lots of things at the moment which he couldn't place or name. Illusion. Vertigo. Significance. Art and life fusing together. Sadness.

'Coming with?' Garuda lifted an eyebrow. The Ethnic Writer looked conflicted. Garuda had enjoyed his garrulous company, perhaps he too had been lonelier than he cared to admit. But the Ethnic Writer seemed more an encumbrance now – a dead weight – than someone who could be helpful.

'I suppose so,' the Ethnic Writer said. 'You don't mind?'

Garuda shrugged. The Ethnic Writer took one last look at the world he knew as he climbed onto Garuda's broad back, and strangely, the words *last port of call* skimmed across his mind.

For eight days and eight nights they flew north. The air progressively became colder. The cold air felt like knives. The sky turned a mellow purple like a giant bruise. The elephant and the turtle rode on Garuda's back, and at nights, the Ethnic Writer snuggled in with them for body-heat. His heart surged with tremulous hope. He looked forward to the crack of dawn. He'd never seen anything so beautiful as the sun rising over the horizon of water and sky. The half-light cast a bluish tinge over the sea they traveled above. The sun was a bright orange fireball against this bluish background. The winds combed his hair and clothes back in powerful gusts. The more he looked out at the vast expanse of rippling blue the more he could not fathom where the ocean ended and the sky began. It seemed vast and limiting all at the same time. Perhaps this was what the inside of an eggshell looked like. Beyond it the universe was unrecognisable, unknowable. He tried to make out the inner lining of the horizon. It was a thin concave blue line, like the rims of a contact lens peered at from the side. The sky looked peaceful, a carapace for the ravaged sea. The sky looked sheltering though impoverished, a crust liable to crack at extreme pressures. He experienced a series of small epiphanies, like body-tremors, and ideas began to form in his head. 'By Jove, I've got it! Love and honour and pity and pride and compassion and sacrifice. But not just honour, also shame, if you're ethnic. Not just pride, but also compulsion. Not just sacrifice, but also curse. Faulkner, all Faulkner all the time, but angled. That's what an Ethnic Writer does. He comes at things from differentiated angles!' He started scribbling and he only stopped occasionally to eat or to shiver when the air became so cold that the muscles in his hand seized up. And then he employed his Dictaphone, speaking far into the night in a low murmur. To Garuda, it felt like a kind of meditative chant, and it almost put him to sleep. Sometimes, the Ethnic Writer would shout with joy, and say, 'Too de loo de la. Too de loo de la!' The cold was absolutely numbing. The Ethnic Writer wrapped a few of Garuda's giant feathers, thick as fur-rugs, around himself and felt as if he was being hurtled back to a time primordial.

On the seventh day, they sighted snow-covered mountains and glaciers. Majestic, desolate, vast landscapes, jagged peaks alternating with plains of snow, like melting curd-cheese, the sound and fury, the loom of a gigantic wall of ice and then so lonely, a sole crumbling fortress in front of this sheer back-drop of ice-blue snow. The gods are worshipped here, the Ethnic Writer thought, and he struggled to find his breath. It made him remember all sorts of things – his mother feeding him cubes of ice made with mango-scented water, his father boasting about a hybrid of mango (crossed genetically with coconut) he'd created that was the size of bowling balls, his grandmother's coffin and how frightening she looked with cot-ton-swabbed eyes and sewn-shut lips, his first dragon dance, his first kung-fu film, the first time he kissed a girl – her name was Sumathy, with a thick braid of hair curling down her back and lips that tasted of nutmeg. His memories bore the shape of people he'd loved tinged with twilight, and although they were things that had happened, they felt mythological. He un-derstood that stories were there to help him explain the things that couldn't be explained.

Garuda was tireless. He felt it now – the mission felt like pres-sure on his bladder and it was mounting the closer he flew to soma. His back was heavy with its burdens, his heart pounding with his exertions, but there was no turning back. He glided, soared, flapped, dipped, swerved, emptied his bladder. The air currents buoyed him. In the distance, a pair of black-necked cranes climbed the skies. Friends or lovers? They were the only other creatures close enough to observe them.

And then, in front of him, the pyramidal shadow of a mountain rose into the heavens, wraithed in mist and fog and clouds. Without a word, Garuda flew straight towards it. Soma. Even the Ethnic Writer had stopped with his murmurings. He witnessed but had no words for what he saw.

They heard it before they saw it – a zinging and whistling of a hail of arrows flying past their heads followed by fireballs that left jet-trails of vapour and gas in their wake. Garuda's beak opened. They turned their heads back to look. It would have been better if they hadn't. What they saw coming at them at great velocities was an avalanche of hurtling, dizzying meteors, fireballs, thunder, a celestial rain of cosmic debris radiating from somewhere to the east of them.

They saw it coming like a rolled-up explosion, and then they were in the thick of it, and darkness fell even as the mass and density of objects were back-lit by crimson silhouettes, moving, swirling, spinning. All around them was falling ash. It had suddenly become very hot. Garuda let out shrill cries. The Ethnic Writer hunkered down in terror. The air was thick with the smells of gas and heat and dust. Dante's inferno, he thought. Elephant trumpeted and the strength of his blows spiralled some of these meteors from their parabolic trajectories. Turtle's head disappeared entirely.

Without warning, Garuda started to fly in haphazard directions, and sometimes he tilted so dangerously to one side that the Ethnic Writer, the elephant and the turtle were in danger of falling off. They swung by their knuckles in hair-raising ways.

'A present from the gods!' Garuda screeched. 'This is the work of Indra. He's trying to stop us. We must be very near the soma.'

'You failed to mention that we would risk getting incinerated,' the Ethnic Writer whined.

'What kind of writer are you if you think this would be easy peasy lemon squeezy?'

'OK, no need to get personal. But how do you propose we get out of this?'

A juddering shook Garuda's body and rattled the teeth of the Ethnic Writer in his head. 'I've been hit!' Garuda said. The air around them suddenly lit up as if a thousand klieg lights in a stadium had been turned on – and the Ethnic Writer saw that tiny figures were sitting on top of some of the shooting asteroids, cheering, raising their fists and shaking them.

'Indra's thunder bolt!' Garuda said and veered swiftly to the right. More hail of arrows followed their flight.

'Those the bad guys, I take it?' the Ethnic Writer pointed at the tiny figures.

'They are the guardians of soma.'

'Aha.'

Garuda plunged and rose, dipped and listed, trying to outdistance the rain of arrows. Where the arrows hit him, feathers were loosened in tufts, floating like dirigibles in the dense air. Of Indra, the Ethnic Writer saw only his shadow looming in the far horizon – this god of thunder, this Zeus equivalent – his triangular headdress, the lean youthful body, the loincloth and thin legs, mounted on top of an elephant.

They were approaching the mistral mountain. Garuda began to flap his wings energetically, rapidly, and the air around them began to move in concentric circles. The Ethnic Writer had never seen anything like it. Invisible molecules of air began to resemble translucent rings of waves, cresting outward, spreading, lace-like eddies of air and dust beginning to spin and project, turning, twisting like water going down a sinkhole. Garuda had created a mighty whirlwind of dust, and the air around them was writhing and churning and spiralling, and they were buffeted and churned along with it. Everything and every creature was caught up in this mighty tornado, hurled with centrifugal force, whirling round and round, faster and faster.

And then the Ethnic Writer felt them dropping. His stomach rose into his throat, the feeling of whooshing down vertically as his body lifted out of its frame. Garuda swayed and canted. They dropped out of the tornado to find themselves headed straight in the onrush of wind cascading towards a giant cantilevered wheel with metal spokes joined in the center. The metal spokes elongated and retracted. The ends of the spokes were sharp spears. They were headed straight for this eyeteeth at great speed.

Through the moving spokes, the Ethnic Writer glimpsed

two golden cups, top up-ended on bottom, and the rims were jagged. The cups too were shifting up and down, the teeth of the top fitting into the cog-like rim of the bottom with exact precision. 'Holy Mother of God, is that where we're going?' He could see a distant magical glow through the open cracks of the rims as the cups moved apart, which only became stronger the closer they were. Garuda breathed in deep and lengthened the span of his wings. It was now or never. He had a split second to insert his beak between the metal spokes and the cracks of the cups and steal the glow within. If the spokes or the cups closed over his beak as he was doing so, they would be disintegrated into a million smithereens. Sayonara, immortality!

The Ethnic Writer clapped both hands over his eyes, peering through his fingers. At that instant, the elephant and turtle catapulted forward and were swallowed up in Garuda's huge maw, vanishing as if they'd never been. This was Death – you often didn't see it coming. The Ethnic Writer's heart jolted in shock. They had meant something to each other, all of them. He swallowed, wondering what his fate would be.

Garuda's wings were perfectly still. They hovered just before these moving spokes. So close that the Ethnic Writer could see that the walls of the cups were uneven, caulked like plaster. A split second later, and the teeth were upon them, and Garuda's head disappeared from view. The Ethnic Writer looked up – he was dangling right in the centre of this metallic jaw – above, he saw fangs gleaming like blades of a guillotine swinging down and the Ethnic Writer felt his heart leap out of its metaphoric cage. *Oh, indelible image seared into my brain. Oh death, here it comes.* And then, the Ethnic Writer felt their retreat. He opened his eyes. Garuda had done it – his beak was entirely cauled in a luminous glow, as yellow as egg-yolk, as phosphorescent as moon jellyfish.

'Yahoo!' The Ethnic Writer couldn't resist. He shrieked with pent-up testosterone and emotion. They were already gliding swiftly away. He turned back towards the wheel and the cups for one last look, and there, arrayed in front of the gasping wheel, were dozens of little figures with ornate headdresses and bracelets around their arms and legs, clad only in loincloths. The gods of soma were watching them depart with their stolen booty, solemn and still. It had been written that this day would come to pass. Many things had been pre-ordained this way, but some weren't. This too Garuda understood.

They flew night and day, over lands, mountains, sea, heading for Garuda's mother. These were mythical lands, ancestral places, and the Ethnic Writer thought he saw similarities with the earth he knew –the taiga, the tundra and the steppes. They evoked feelings of longing and homesickness and nostalgia in the Ethnic Writer (even though he'd never seen these places on earth with his own eyes).

And then, they heard music, a lone flute. Playful then sad, haunting then not, lilting then erratic. It was a ballad of antonyms. It was calling Garuda by his essence. Garuda lifted his beak, and his eyes closed for a second. He too remembered his mother telling stories, stroking his hair, grooming his feathers. Stories about her evil twin Kadru. Stories about mortals.

A large cloud drifting by above cast a sullen shadow over them. Both of them glanced up simultaneously. It was Indra with his thunderbolt, hovering in the airspace on the back of an elephant, looking contrite and accommodating.

'Well, hello. Fancy catching up with you like this.'

Garuda frowned. With the soma in his beak, he really wasn't equipped to speak. He gestured at the Ethnic Writer with his beak towards Indra.

'Me?' the Ethnic Writer stammered. 'Ehm… what do you…' He cleared his throat for a more authoritative voice. 'What do you want?'

Indra flashed them a snaggle-toothed grin. 'There's really no point in us being enemies. You have soma. Which is fine. Really. I thought I should tell you though that you mustn't let the snakes have it.'

The Ethnic Writer looked at Garuda. Garuda flapped one wing, thinking quickly. He gestured at the Ethnic Writer's notepad and wrote down, 'Tell him it's to ransom my mother.'

'It's to ransom his mother.' The Ethnic Writer snuck one hand under his armpit for comfort.

'I understand that,' said Indra with some impatience. 'All he has to do is deliver the soma to the snakes. They don't have to possess it, know what I mean?'

They hadn't known. Garuda felt a trick in the offing. He felt his confidence wavering. Indra was king of the gods after all. Kings often knew what they were talking about. Or so one hoped.

'Let's strike a deal,' Indra said. 'What say I give you something as consideration? What do you want?'

Garuda was always hungry. He was also dead nervous about accidentally eating a Brahman. He thought for a bit and selected his next words carefully, wrote them down carefully. 'Ask him if I may eat all the snakes.'

The Ethnic Writer smiled. 'May he please eat all the snakes?'

'Sure,' Indra was equally expansive. 'Why not? No skin off my nose.'

'I would also like to study the Vedas,' Garuda wrote.

The Ethnic Writer parroted. Indra's grin widened, 'Done!'

And then, like that, the Ethnic Writer knew what Indra was up to.

They could see the snakes down in the mosh pit below, coils upon coils upon coils of writhing black slinkiness, slithering, constantly moving. The Ethnic Writer shuddered.

'Throw it upon that dharba grass over there!' Indra yelled. They both saw him fly off with this last instruction. Garuda cast out the soma from his beak, and it dribbled like a basketball across the valley onto a thatch of grass that was a different shade from its surroundings. Immediately when the soma came to rest on it, the grass turned a golden yellow. Each blade of grass opened up to reveal a scurrying and bustling of thousands of movements – little people everywhere – gods, celestial beings, baubles of spirit, all inhabiting a briefly transparent realm. The Ethnic Writer blinked in incredulity.

The snakes began to writhe towards the soma as a body. It was like the flow of black lava, cresting with different heads.

'Before you touch the soma, you have to have a purification bath!' Garuda screeched. The snakes halted. Nothing moved and there could be heard only the rustle of the wind. Distantly, they could still hear the flute, or its echo. Just as miraculously, it worked. The course of this black wave changed. It headed towards the river. Garuda led the way, ensuring no snake slid away from the pack.

The soma was left alone on the grass. The Ethnic Writer couldn't explain why he did what he did next. It was impulse. It was the loss of oneself. With a horrific yell, he leapt from Garuda's back. 'Keep going! I'll see you later. Enjoy your snakes!'

He saw the soma. Still resplendent. Still glowing. Then. The Giant Hand coming down from above. Swiftly descending.

'Nooooooo!' The Ethnic Writer had nothing with him to stop Indra stealing back the soma. His heart knocked crazily, his knees buckled, his eyes misted, but his hands threw up all those pages of his notepad, those pages filled with his chicken-scrawly writing, filled with ideas and nubs of ideas and line upon literal line of nonsensical words he'd written during their journey north. He'd thought they were finer than anything he'd ever written and also the least meaningful of anything he'd ever written.

The Hand swept these pages aside. It curled into a Fist and came down and hammered the Ethnic Writer in one mighty blow. His breath left him and he lay there with his eyes open, then shut. He imagined he saw Garuda circling back towards him, wings extended, having consumed all the snakes. But the sky was empty, as blank and white as a baby's blanket. He hadn't done enough to warn Garuda.

He watched Indra lift the soma in his hand and ride away, triumphant.

Knowledge came to him of failure and inability. The Ethnic Writer took in a deep breath and it was painful; the sun was directly in his eyes, and his vision dimmed, trailing a dusky halo. He tried to hold his breath in but that hurt too. Words came to him. *Puny mortals metamorphose into pentameters.* Ha ha. A poem called *Shifting the Sun* – parts of it. *Who wrote this?*

When your father dies, say the French, you become your own father.

He lay there imagining his own death. For one moment, as his lungs wheezed he thought he was dying. But no, he'd merely been thoroughly flattened. Lost to himself, lost to the world. His eyes focused on the white sheets of paper sailing in the sky, fluttering, pages and pages of confetti, *was someone getting married? Was there a plane in the sky?* But no, it wasn't paper confetti. And nothing mattered any more. There'd been only one word that he had scrawled floating back in front of his dim eyes – it came out of nowhere.

Light.

But did it mean the absence of darkness or the absence of weight?

Household Gods

Tracy Fells

Mohammed placed the cube of lamb into the ceramic dish, its minty aroma mingling with the hint of cranberry and cinnamon from the lighted candle. He'd bought a range of Christmas spiced tea lights in the January sales, which would help to keep Vesta's flame alight. When he had to leave the house, Mo blew it out, not trusting Vesta's naked flame alone with his mother.

Into the second dish he poured a libation of elderflower cordial. 'Accept my offerings, Janus, and help to ease the ending I face today,' he whispered, eyes open and fixed on the home-made shrine. Typically he sought Vesta's blessing, as protector of the home and family, before leaving the house, but Mo felt that the sad and difficult day ahead required additional support. He repeated the request six more times under his breath.

Later he would bring cake for his household gods. He was a good son, but a poor Muslim, and had promised his mother he would bring home a cake: Victoria sponge, with real jam, her favourite, to celebrate the prophet's birthday. Today he would also visit the hospital to see the baby for the first, and possibly last, time; born on the first day of the year and now twenty-four days old. Not a day for celebrations.

Despite not eating meat since he was nine years old, the same age he'd discovered his true faith, Mo wrinkled his nose approvingly at the tempting smell of the minted lamb. After finishing his morning shift at Meadowbank garden centre Mo had chopped and spoon-fed the rest of the steak, along with garlic mash and home grown petit pois, to Mummy. He liked to see her eat a good lunch before he set off for the library. Friday afternoons, his one afternoon off, were for study and the world-wide-web was his undisputed god of research. He didn't own a computer; at two o'clock each Friday he would take his place at one of the public terminals in the town's library.

The telephone call, coming as Mo helped his mother waddle back from the commode, exploded his afternoon plans and summoned him to the hospital. Mo checked his pulse, ninety-eight and rising, but could not ignore the clipped vowels of the duty nurse who instructed him to come *immediately* and say goodbye to his daughter.

Extinguishing Vesta's flame he bowed towards the shrine, eyes closed, to murmur a final prayer. He kept the shrine in his bedroom so as not to upset Mummy. Mo had created his design from photographs he'd found on the Internet of a typical Roman household shrine. The finished relief appeared authentic with its weathered (cold coffee worked a treat) columns and sloping roof chiselled from modelling plaster. First tracing with heavy pencil the dancing figures and the writhing snake, Mo later coloured-in the sketches using a tin of watercolour paints he found in an attic crate of his old toys and books. Balanced on the apex of the shrine was a stone statue, with two faces, both adorned with long curling beards. The god Janus, protector of doors and gateways, was often represented by two heads to signify how he could simultaneously watch both the past and the future. Mo didn't envy the god this talent, as he could barely think about the past let alone face the future.

If Mo had made an offering to give thanks for the baby's birth then maybe he wouldn't now have to make the torturous visit to her hospital incubator - to stand with Aisha and pretend to grieve for another man's child.

Mo selected a TV channel showing an afternoon of black and white films, tucked the blanket of crocheted squares around his mother's legs, and kissed her dry forehead.

'I have to go out, Mummy,' he said clearly to her blank face, 'I will ask Mrs Harris to pop in later and make you more tea. You like your afternoon tea, don't you, Mummy?'

She blinked, as if in acknowledgement, but her dark eyes looked past him. Pulling the curtains across, to keep the heat in, Mo flicked the light switch on and off seven times before crossing the threshold. He quietly closed the door to his mother's sitting room and repeated the action with the kitchen, downstairs cloakroom and hall lights. The front door was safely chained and double-locked, so he let himself out through the kitchen door. He locked and unlocked the door six times and then after a quick prayer invoking the blessing of Janus he locked it one final time.

Mo dropped the key into Mrs Harris' shaking hand, being careful not to brush against her fingers.

'Yes, dear,' she chirped, 'I know how Mrs Khan likes her tea. I'll look in on her after the three o'clock at Chepstow. Now she won't need the loo or anything, will she?'

He shook his head. Mo was below average height, but he still looked down at his neighbour, the tight white curls of her perm hugging her scalp in the snapping easterly wind.

'She went after lunch,' he said starting to back away from the old lady.

'Oh, that's lovely, dear.' There was a splash of lipstick on a lower tooth and the cherry-red hadn't made it all the way round her cracked lips. 'Your mother is rather a big-boned lady.'

With older women, particularly white English ladies, Mo always felt the need to end an interaction with a slight bow. He did this now to hide the twitch of a smile. He knew Mrs Khan's bones were no bigger than any other Pakistani woman of her age, but they were significantly well insulated.

Mrs Harris stretched out her arm, almost as if she were about to stroke his head, but then pulled it back to her chest.

'God be with you,' she whispered and then scuffled back inside her house.

Which god, thought Mo, when there were so many to choose from? Two days after his ninth birthday Mohammed had woken to find Uncle Osman, nicknamed Oz, squatting at the edge of his bed, tears rolling down his shiny cheeks. Usually he had the smiling appearance of a garden Buddha, but that night Uncle Oz sagged like a deflating rubber ring. He gurgled and spluttered and finally spat out a story involving a lorry, a moped and Mo's father's delivery van. There was no happy ending to the bedtime tale. Mo buried the details of his uncle's words and accepted that his father was gone. He had left them for good. Uncle Oz told Mo he had to pray to God, pray for his father. But what was the point of prayers for a dead man?

At nine years old Mo had decided one god wasn't enough. If you were to protect and keep safe all those you loved you needed a whole battalion. Multiple prayers to multiple deities distributed your fielders across a dangerous pitch. At least one of them should always be there, in place to take that fateful catch. In school his class had been working on an art project to recreate a floor mosaic from a Roman villa. Mo devoured the books his teacher had brought in for inspiration, feasting on the gory history of Julius Cesar and the Emperors that followed, but mostly he was impressed by the cautious nature of the ancients. The Romans hedged all their bets by spreading their wishes and prayers across a multitude of gods. Jupiter was top god, the Headmaster, with his goddess wife Juno followed by Minerva and Mars, and too many others to list all taking responsibility for a key area of daily life. Mo adopted their beliefs because it was the perfect religious contingency, removing risk and misery from his fragile existence.

He also reasoned that his father, when leaving the safety and sanctuary of the family home, had left himself open to the fates. Crossing the threshold from inside to out was a dangerous undertaking. By his tenth birthday Mo had developed numerous strategies to cope with the challenge of endless doorways.

Mo continued with his beliefs and little rituals that had begun after his father's death. However, according to Uncle Oz, a single man over thirty needed a wife. After Mummy's second, and more debilitating, stroke Mo could no longer cope with her alone and continue to work at the garden centre. Several carer visits were scheduled each day to help bathe and feed Mrs Khan while Mo was working. Uncle Oz reasoned a wife would be a more permanent solution – and cheaper.

Uncle Oz took care of all the arrangements and Aisha was shipped to Sussex. She came from a good family, known to his uncle, and brought with her one small suitcase of clothes. Mo's new wife spoke no English and after five months living in the provincial suburbs had made little progress with her vocabulary. With Uncle Oz she'd spoken only Urdu. To Mo she said little more than 'Good morning, husband' and 'Good night, husband', recited and learned from Uncle Oz. After the wedding, Mo moved to the spare bedroom and painted Aisha's room a pale lemon, a colour chosen to complement her favourite sari.

Mo always made an effort to tell his mother about his day at Meadowbank nursery, talking to her was excellent therapy, or so he'd been told. She did not respond.

One evening, after an unexpected late shift at Meadowbank, Mo arrived home to find Aisha sitting with his mother. He watched the two women from beyond the kitchen door as Aisha spoon-fed his mother from a bowl of soup chatting happily away in Urdu about her life before England. Aisha talked of her younger brothers and sisters and their silly pranks. She was funny. Her eyes were bright, her smile relaxed. Her long ebony hair, usually tightly pinned in a coil at the back of her head, hung loose across both shoulders. Mo crept up to his bedroom, leaving his wife undisturbed by his return.

Now Aisha was at the hospital, where she visited every day since the birth. Mo would be a dutiful husband and take his place at her side.

After reversing the car from the garage Mo parked on the drive and returned to the house. He tugged on the front door and then the kitchen door; they were both secure, finally murmuring some words of thanks to Vesta he climbed back into the grey hatchback.

*

Mo spoke his name clearly into the box on the wall. A buzzer trilled and the glass-fronted door clicked open. Inside the Special Care Unit a middle-aged nurse, wearing pristine white, escorted him to a corner room suffused with light. Winding an elastic band in her fingers the nurse pulled her blond hair into a ponytail, instantly making her look ten years younger. Turning on her heels, the ponytail almost slapping his face, the nurse strode off again, leaving Mo alone outside the door.

Mo peered through the round window, unsure if he could enter without an escort. Six incubators sat inside like elevated greenhouse trays. Three of them were watched over by electronic displays and hushed couples. By the fourth sat Aisha, her hands held in the lap of her sari, her head bowed.

'Mr Khan?' A sharp, female voice came from behind him. Another nurse, this one wore a navy-blue uniform, squinted at him with dark, narrow eyes.

'Yes,' he answered backing up against the door, 'but please call me Mo.'

'Your English is excellent, Mr Khan. I'm surprised because your wife can hardly speak a word. Thankfully, one of the ward porters speaks Urdu and he's translated anything we needed to know from her.' Her tone was scolding, making Mo feel he was the source of her irritation.

Mo wanted to counter, gently state he was as English as the next man, born in Brighton General and living in Sussex all his life, but the next man, jogging past in a flapping white coat, called out with an antipodean accent for someone to hold the main door. Instead, Mo replied, 'My wife has only lived here for a short time.'

One silver-grey eyebrow twitched as the older nurse sucked on her lip. 'Your wife's vigil, Mr Khan, has been lonely. But you're here now and your company will ease the waiting.'

He followed the blue nurse into the incubator room. The rhythmic sigh of oxygen pumps and the infrequent beep of some machine were the only background sounds. Aisha stood as her husband approached. Her gaze flicked from him to settle again on the brown skinned baby lying beneath a Perspex roof.

The nurse spoke behind him. 'A prem baby is particularly susceptible to infections, Mr Khan, we've treated the pneumonia as best we can but now it is –'

'– In the lap of the gods?' said Mo quietly

'Simply down to the strength of your daughter's immune system,' she finished.

He didn't see her leave, but the starched blue nurse was replaced by the smiling nurse in white, who stood so close Mo could smell antiseptic and cigarette smoke on her skin. She squeezed his hand.

In the men's toilets Mo lathered his hands and wrists with soap, then rinsed them in the tepid water. Five times would be sufficient, he thought, but returned to the sink to wash twice more.

Walking back to the incubator room Mo passed the open kitchen area where the navy-blue nurse stood, her back towards him, talking with a male colleague. 'Poor mare, shipped over here and nobody cares enough to give her the tools to survive.' Her voice carried above the stirring teaspoon of her colleague. 'Told Jamal she was in love, that she had a boyfriend back in Pakistan – a medical student. But his family didn't approve or something and she was the one that had to leave. I feel sorry for her, dumped with a bloke she's never met and expected to start spitting out babies like chapattis.'

The male nurse inclined his head towards Mo and the woman slowly twisted round to stare at him. She sipped at the mug in her hands, but didn't offer an apology.

He could leave now; drive home and get on with dinner. Mummy needed to eat before the temporary carer arrived to bathe her before bedtime. His duty at the hospital had been executed, he'd seen the baby as requested – what more was there for him to do? Aisha wasn't going anywhere, so his presence was irrelevant.

The smiling nurse held open the door to the incubator room and gestured to Mo, 'Are you coming back in, Mo?'

A strand of blond hair had slipped free to dangle across her cheek. Mo needed to see her push it back into place, but she kept the door open with her backside unaware of her unbalanced hair.

'No,' he said, deciding quickly, 'not yet.'

Something flashed in her blue eyes, like the reflected glint of a flame. She was beautiful, Mo realised, quite beautiful. 'A child is always a blessing,' she said. A frown creased her forehead, yet the words were tender and soothed him.

Beyond the sliding doors of the main reception Mo turned his mobile back on. A man in a striped dressing gown leant against a pillar taking long drags from a cigarette; his other hand supported the stand of his drip with the tube still attached, disappearing up his sleeve. The sky looked tired, drained of light. Clouds hung low, grey and brooding, swollen with the promise of snow.

*

The baby was another man's child. Mo was certain on the paternity of Aisha's daughter because of two things. Firstly, his new wife had landed at Heathrow already three months pregnant, Uncle Oz confessed this before her arrival, and secondly he had never slept in her bed. Mo lost his virginity during his teenage bacchanalian phase, a time of experimentation and too much vodka. Alison, with hair the colour of copper piping, let him *do it* at the end of school party in her parent's room. He was sixteen and had already starting working at the garden centre. There were, occasionally, other girls after Alison but Mo had not yet consummated his marriage with Aisha. She was a stranger to him. After Mummy's first stroke his affliction had worsened to the point where Mo could barely tolerate the touch of another human being.

The man with the drip raised his eyebrows and nodded, tossing Mo a silent *alright mate*. Mo turned away to stare across the car park where an ambulance was backing towards the doors of A and E.

'Mrs Harris?' he spoke into his mobile. He turned up the

volume to hear the old lady's whispery voice. 'Oh, good, I'm glad Mrs Khan enjoyed her afternoon tea. Could I possibly ask another favour, Mrs Harris?' Snow was falling now. 'Yes, I will be here for some hours. If you could sit with…' Drip man stubbed his cigarette against the concrete pillar and let it fall. Specks of snow began to settle on the tarmac. 'Mummy, Mrs Khan, loves soup – thank you. Yes, I will let my wife know you are praying for our daughter.'

A child is always a blessing.

Mo shut down the phone. How did Mrs Harris know the baby was a girl? He'd never talked about Aisha's baby with Mrs Harris. Had Aisha learned more English than he realised?

His right hand was shaking. Mo hadn't changed out of his work clothes, so still wore the green uniform of the garden centre: drill trousers, polo shirt, sweatshirt and the ivy-green fleece with Meadowbank's red and gold logo. It was the cold of course; he was bound to shiver, standing inert outside in a snowstorm. As the doors slid open Mo saw himself in the glass, a short brown man in shabby green. His father had been lost for twenty-five years, but was now returned to them. Mo saw him all the time, whenever he faced his own reflection. The same receding hairline, the swelling bald spot racing to meet his forehead, and the same fearful eyes were all part of the inheritance. He held a finger under his nose. All he needed was a neatly trimmed moustache and his father would be fully resurrected.

Did Janus watch over sliding doors? As the god of doorways he must lurk nearby, never dropping his guard no matter who entered.

Drip man shuffled past. 'The gods walk amongst us,' said the man, staring straight ahead. From the back his thick neck bulged, prickled with stubble, almost like a second chin.

'Excuse me, what did you say?'

The man stopped, turning to blink at Mo. 'Sorry, mate, didn't say nothing.'

'My mistake,' said Mo.

*

Aisha had been crying. A paper towel lay scrunched in her lap and dark lines creased her eyelids. The incubator was open and for the first time Mo peered into the baby's self-contained world. A nappy hung off the baby's bony hips. From her nose protruded a plastic tube, taped across her tummy. She wore one pink, hand knitted mitten, on her right hand. The other was bare and the fingers twitched in time with the rise and fall of her chest.

'You can hold her hand if you wish.' The nurse in white was once again at Mo's side. He glanced at her and she nodded. 'There's little she can catch from you that will do any more harm than pneumococcus.'

Before he could prepare himself the baby's hand curled around his finger. Her grip was surprisingly strong. His breathing raced to match his heartbeat, but he was determined not to pull away from her touch. Mo gazed at the creases on her coffee skin, the baby's hand looked like his own, a perfect replica, but in miniature.

'Why is she wearing a mitten?' said Mo.

'To stop her pulling out the tube. Aisha expresses her milk and we feed baby through the tube, it goes straight into her stomach. She is a bit small, and weak, to feed by mouth.'

'But why only one mitten?'

Her expression softened. 'Somehow she lost the other one before you came in. We can't find it anywhere.'

Mo recalled the telephone message he'd picked up earlier. The navy-blue nurse was called Julia, now he remembered. 'Julia told me she may not last the night, that she is very weak.'

'So many of them try to grow wings, but I believe your little girl wants to stay. Do you have a name for her?'

Would a name anchor her? Weigh down her wings? A nagging voice whispered inside his head, his mother's voice. She cannot meet God without a name.

Another voice spoke to him, Aisha's quiet voice. 'Nadira.'

'Nadira, after my mother?'

Aisha nodded.

'This baby is a rare and precious gift; let her bring love into your home.' The nurse's words unfurled around them like an embrace. Mo looked away from Aisha, but the pony-tailed woman had already slipped away. Mo didn't know the nurse's name, as she hadn't worn a nametag. She didn't return to say goodbye at the end of her shift and he never saw her again in the unit.

'You've been very helpful to Mummy,' Mo said in Urdu to Aisha.

'I wish I'd known her before the stroke. I think we would have become friends.'

Mo hesitated, swallowing several times. 'I think she likes you very much.' He thought of how Aisha read to her every day, of how she fed Mummy, waiting patiently for each mouthful to go down before gently offering another.

A hint of a smile crept onto Aisha's face. Her black eyes met his briefly then swept back to the baby. She wasn't conventionally pretty, her face a little too thin and pointed, but her eyes were kind. 'I think she has a good son,' said Aisha softly. 'A kind and loving son.'

He thought of what he'd overheard outside the nurse's kitchen. 'You don't have to stay. You could go home… after.' Mo stopped. There were no appropriate words to frame his meaning.

Aisha shook her head and replied carefully in English. 'I want to stay.' She reached forward to stroke her baby's chest and began to talk again in Urdu. 'This is our home now. We will stay if you wish us to. I will ask nothing more of you.'

Together they stood beside the incubator, watching over Nadira.

Snowflakes funnelled towards the windows like desperate white moths. The ticking machines and wheezing babies settled to a low, constant hum, as Mo began to recite his prayer. He didn't care which of the gods heard it – he knew they were all listening. Nadira snuffled like a kitten in her incubator, pawing at the feeding tube with her mittened hand, still tightly holding onto Mo's finger with the other.

*

At dawn, Mo drove Aisha home. Overnight the snow had blown away and the roads were clear. They both planned to bathe and eat, before returning to the hospital to continue the vigil at their daughter's side. The budding wings had faded with the snow as the antibiotics finally kicked in. Baby Nadira was staying for now.

Mummy was lying on her back, a rattling snore told Mo she was still sleeping. Mrs Harris had spent the night, squashing in beside Mrs Khan to teeter at the edge of the counterpane. The old lady was also asleep; the white curls around her ear were stuck flat against the pillow and her face.

He returned to his own bedroom. It was time to give thanks to the household gods.

Someone had beaten him to it. Vesta's flame was alive and flickering before Mo's plaster shrine. He had extinguished the candle, and checked it seven times before leaving for the hospital, but now the candle was burning in its dish. Beside it lay a single pink woollen mitten.

A Moment Could Last Them Forever

Dan Carpenter

She has inherited her father's gift, in her own way.

The streetlamp buzzes outside, and the rattle of a bus tinkles the spoon on the saucer. She grips hold of her tea. Her client totters in with a plate of cakes, store bought, and smiles a wrinkle-creased smile.

'Here.' She offers the plate. 'Guests have the first pick.'

Her name is Edna, she lives alone and got in touch through the church group. There are always whispers from the church group, a drifting of recommendation. Often they just want to speak to a loved one: husband, brother, father; sometimes it's a celebrity and sometimes, when she's really lucky, they want to know their futures. Not that any of them have much of one. Her circuit, if it can be called as much, is the living rooms, kitchens and conservatories of the retired, ill and lonely. She doesn't talk to the dead, not in the way her father did, although she privately jokes to herself that her clients tend to be close enough.

She takes the plate from Edna and picks a cake as though selecting a weapon in a dual to the death.

'I want to speak to my Victor,' Edna says, 'I want to know if he's happy, and if he hears me when I speak to him.' She picks up her tea, hands shaking, and touches the rim of the mug to her lips, tilting it slightly, carefully. She looks pale, her skin thinning, losing colour. 'Can you help me?'

'I do things different, did they tell you that?'

'Yes, they said something like that.'

'I don't do Ouija boards or séances or anything. Now, do you have it?'

Edna nods, and stands again. 'It's in the kitchen, I did like you said on the phone; seven days?'

'Yes, that should do it.'

Edna leaves the room again. The older crowd, her only crowd really, tend not to produce the best results. She remembers doing this at University: lines scrawled across enormous maps of the city, strange sigils along roads, by-ways, motorways, and riversides. The most recent in still-wet ink, and the oldest a fading black, the ink drying and dying. She shudders, thinking about those years, doing readings at house parties, being the weird girl. Edna comes back in, and it is immediately clear that this isn't going to be the wildest of readings. She has a small fold out road-map of Hither Green. The road they are on, scribbled on several times with a black pen, scratching a deep groove into the page. The line leads from the house, up the road to the high street, the supermarket, and the church.

'As you can tell, I don't get out much,' Edna explains. She hasn't yet taken a piece of cake for herself.

'That's fine, don't worry. It'll still work. The most important thing is that we don't lie; it doesn't work if we lie. As long as this is a real week for you, and represents everywhere you went, we can work with it.' There is no answer, so she assumes Edna is telling the truth. She takes a blank piece of paper from her bag, and several marker pens, and then removes the light box: a part from an old projector she found in the dump.

'Have you got a socket?'

She places the map on the light box and switches it on. It buzzes louder than the streetlamp outside, and she can feel the heat coming off it already. She unfolds the map as far as she can and places it on top of the box, the light barely shines through, but the lines are clearly lit up. She places the blank, opaque sheet of paper over the top of the map, and the lines bleed through underneath like shadows. She pauses for a moment, her hand wavering over the selection of marker pens, and she picks a medium thick one first, tracing the line from Edna's home, down the road to the high street. A daily trip by the looks of it, an arterial vessel, with little capillary veins running out to the other places, trailing away. She takes a thinner pen for those. Edna doesn't say much whilst she recreates the map. Sometimes they comment on their activities. *That's when my son took me out for dinner.* Or, *I go dancing every Thursday: ballroom.* She feels sorry for Edna, and wonders whether she even wants any of this, whether all she wants is some company.

'Have you got a bowl? Something you don't mind getting burned?'

'Burned? What are you going to do? I don't want my net curtains catching.'

'It won't spread. I've done this plenty of times before.' She switches the light box off, and holds up the piece of paper, the lines now out of context, an inverted L with tiny spidery tendrils running off. 'It's a kind of sigil,' she explains. 'Think of it like static, do you know about static electricity? Like a Van De Graff. You run it and it builds up and builds up until you release the energy. It's a bit like that. You can build up and build up all these thoughts about yourself, or anyone over the week, and this shape here...' She holds the piece of paper up so Edna can see. '... is a symbol of all that built up energy. All we have to do is release it.'

'And the fire will do that?'

'Oh yes, burning works spectacularly.'

Edna brings a bowl from the kitchen and places it in the middle of the table. She holds on to it for just a moment, as though considering whether she really wants to ruin the bowl, and eventually lets go.

'Here.' She passes Edna the piece of paper. 'Put that in the bowl, and then we set fire to it. It was your husband wasn't it? That's who you wanted to contact?' Edna nods. 'Okay then, just keep him in your mind. Is there something you remember strongly about him? Something significant?'

'He wore Old Spice.'

'Just keep thinking about that.' Edna shuts her eyes tight. 'No, no, you can keep your eyes open. I need you to place the paper in the bowl, if you keep your eyes shut, you might miss it.' She snaps them open again and picks up the piece of paper, lowering it into the bowl.

'Here,' she hands the lighter to Edna, 'It's best if you light it.'

After, she smokes outside in Edna's garden. The grass is a little overgrown, and when she walks through it, pacing as she always does, she can feel the wetness of dew from the unmowed grass seep into her tights, ankle high. She turns to look at the house, the dim light from the living room flickers. The rumble of traffic is lessening as the night bears down. She can see Edna in the house, sat in the chair, crying silently, but she is just a faded kind of shadow. There are no stars out, just a thick cloud. She's heard that there's a gale coming, although the night is still. Edna opens the backdoor. 'Do you want another cup of tea?' She doesn't appear to be shaken. She has promised Edna that she'll do it again, at no extra cost, in a week or so. She doesn't think that it will do any good. It's the journey. There is a rustling in the bushes, probably a fox or a cat, and she stubs her cigarette out, heads back inside the house, and leaves immediately.

A week has not added much to Edna's journeying.

'I tried to head out a bit more,' she said, passing over the map. 'Of course, I had to go to the bookstore to buy a new roadmap, but because I didn't have it with me, I didn't mark it up, should I have done? Will this not work again?'

'I shouldn't think that would matter.' She thinks it might, but she won't say anything.

Edna has coated the room in Old Spice, his last bottle apparently. 'You said it would help,' she explains. 'I've been listening to his old records. Couldn't bring myself to wear his clothes though. Got out one of his old jumpers and put my arm through the sleeve, but it felt like it was too far.'

They repeat the procedure and again, the results are timid at best. Last week she was sure she heard a low moan coming from inside the bowl, a coming of *something*, and this week: not even that. There may, she concedes afterwards with Edna, have been a flash of purple light, but that may have just been one of the party limos ferrying twenty-something girls to a hen party somewhere in the city.

'I don't want you to get your hopes up,' she says to Edna, 'this isn't an exact science.'

She leaves Edna's, promising to return next week; knowing it will still not work. 'Maybe,' she says, 'you should get out some photos of him. Try to think back to the times you spent with him. Maybe that will help build up a good atmosphere.'

'Do you think he might not be here? That maybe he's just

gone for good? Am I not good enough to haunt?' Edna has plenty of questions.

'I'm sure he's here,' she says, and to reinforce it she places her hand on Edna's arm. She wonders if it all seems too forced. She remembers something her father said, 'To know that they're not alone for a moment, that could last them forever.' Edna shuts the door leaving her standing in the unlit porch. She trudges back to the bus stop, her bag weighing her down.

She has other clients. There is the milkman who is sure his mother occupies the welsh-dresser, rattling the thin, delicate china; and drinking the gin. There is the young just-married couple, frightened to sleep at night for the thing that lies in bed, keeping them apart. Then, there is the middle-aged woman, who cries on her shoulder about her young son, as they burn her little tube map in a mixing bowl. They, all of them, work. There are results and endings. When she leaves, they tell her that she has changed their lives, that they will be happier. She can't help but think of Edna.

Later in the week: Edna phones her in the middle of the night. She answers the phone half asleep, waking from a dream about a meal she has been eating inside her father's stomach.

'I think I heard him,' Edna wails from the other end.

'You didn't hear him.'

'He said, *I miss you Eddie, I miss you,* and then he smashed the glass that had my false teeth in.'

'I don't think he said that.'

'I think now might be the perfect time, can you come to the house now? I've got the map handy.'

She looks at her bedside clock. The streetlamp outside her window has broken again, so the clock is the only source of light in the room.

'It's half four in the morning.'

'I really think this is what was missing. I can pay you double. I just want to speak to him one more time.'

'Good night.'

She lies still in her bed, staring up at the ceiling where the paper peels away from a damp patch, eager to escape. She wonders if maybe she could pretend to get in touch with Edna's husband, just a little flight of fancy. Rig a wire to knock a cup over, or plant a tape recorder with some garbled Hallmark message in. Just thinking about it makes her shudder. She had seen the frauds at play in darkened theatres; with earpieces and assistants. At least she had the courage to admit when it wasn't working, although, there hasn't been anyone she's failed. Not yet. But why is it so difficult for her to get through with Edna?

She tries to sleep, and, as always, dreams of herself stretched thin like wires across the roads near her father's house.

Edna has prepared everything this week.

She arrives promptly, and Edna has already made her a cup of tea. They sit down in the living room. She notices the floor is strewn with photos of Edna's husband: wedding pictures, holiday snaps, and several particularly revealing private shots. Edna is wearing a jumper which clearly belonged to him. She smells of Old Spice (*I bought some more, just for this*). She even looks different. Her face, which had been thin and pale but happy, looks more tired, sadder. It's the same withered, Victorian expression her husband has in the photographs. Edna hands her a bowl of stew.

'It was his favourite,' she explains. 'He always cooked it. I thought it might help.'

It smells rich and warm. Edna hands her a map, this one bigger and more expansive, with side streets and alleys marked out clearly. Her journeys have become wider, far reaching. There are regular trips into the city, lines criss-crossing and intertwining, meandering around the roads like forgotten string. There is no symbol, there is no pattern. This is confusion and fear. This is looking to escape, to run away and hide. This is desperation.

Once, she recorded her own journeys across the city, marking them down on a scrawny map, spindly lines tracing her journey to work and back again. When she looked at it properly at the end of the week she saw a perfectly shaped V. An arrow pointing her away from the city, away from everything. It was then that she got too scared to burn it, too scared to see whatever wanted her to leave, whatever brushed past her hair at night, tilted the paintings on her wall and whatever switched the TV channels over at whim.

She looks at Edna and understands that fear is not always about what is there, lurking in the shadows, but that what is there might not be what you were looking for. That what you were looking for was never there.

That they are gone.

Edna plays her husband's favourite record. The Kinks' 'Village Green Preservation Society'. The needle jumps at first, but then settles in as the music spatters out of the old speakers in the corner. She has the same bowl from the other weeks; the charcoaled remains of the previous attempts still lie in the basin. Edna closes the curtains, and dims the lights.

Her eyes adjust to the lack of light, and she watches Edna take her seat. She flicks the light box on, placing another blank sheet over it, and then begins to outline the shape Edna has created. She finds that, instead of just tracing over it, making it just another shape, it is easier to start at the house on the map, and take the journeys with her. She follows the road down the hill to the train station, and imagines the tip of her pen is waiting at the platform, watching the train pull in slowly, and then sitting in the carriage watching as the blanket terrace houses pass her by as she heads into the city. She follows the line around the streets, into shops and down alleys, she doubles back on herself several times, stopping off in shops and cafes, browsing bookstores, before turning back to the station. The line doesn't head home straight away. Instead, it stops off halfway up, somewhere around London Bridge, and continues along, down the river. This is a filter of a filter of a life. The resulting scribble on the page is not like the previous weeks, it seems muddled and random: there is no symbol, nothing that seems to hold any meaning. She looks up at Edna, who is wringing her hands to stop them from shaking.

She passes her the sheet of paper and Edna places it in the bowl, and then lights it.

When she lights her cigarette outside, the wind has died down and there is a calm in the garden. A solitary cardigan hangs from a washing line in front of her, and somewhere nearby, next door perhaps, there is the hollow sound of someone moving a wheelie-bin. She feels relief for the first time in weeks. Edna is sat in her chair in the living room. The pictures have settled and the bowl has crashed spectacularly to the floor, the ash rising from the splinters and forming rudimentary words and pictures in the air, before disintegrating. There was a voice, and although all she heard was a vague murmur, Edna swears it was her dear husband. More power to her.

As she sits smoking, a small fox treads through the grass, finding its way into the garden through a gap in the wall next to her. It's young and its thin, lithe body slinks across the garden. It stops halfway across and stares at her. Under the moon, the fox casts strange shadows so that its body appears twisted, and its arms and legs are stretched and elongated. She watches it. The two of them keep their eyes on one another for what seems like forever. Then, it turns and walks away, and she holds her finger up and traces its path across the garden, memorising the shape and immortalising it.

Take Away the Sky

Mark Mayes

It began with a man standing halfway across a bridge.

The sun was going down over the valley. The trees below the bridge were darkening, swaying in the evening breeze.

That afternoon he'd drawn a Tarot card that told him to watch his back, that slander and malicious intent lay at his seemingly peaceful periphery – no doubt seeking a breach through which to enter. That breach might be fostered by forgetfulness, contentment, a fading of vigilance among these apparently easier days. Enemies are often near, although they may be distal and residing in unknown territory, plotting, setting the dominoes a-tumbling.

He leant slightly, not too much, over the white railings. From this point, a good one-hundred-and-twenty-foot drop.

The fag-end of the rush hour crossed the bridge at ever wider intervals. Workers coming home from one or other of two cities, heading for dinner, telly, bed.

A young woman had jumped, or fallen, from this very bridge only a few weeks back. She went over less than six feet from where the man now stood, leaning, eyes half closed, allowing the cooling air to smooth his thoughts.

For the first ten days, a bunch of flowers had been tied with blue ribbon to one of the upright struts of the railing. Carnations. One particular night's storm had done for them, sent them scattering into the valley through the treetops. The loop of blue ribbon remained, fallen to ground level, dirty now. The man hadn't noticed it.

Neither had he heard about the young woman's demise, as he'd recently been away and receiving treatment for what's now, humanely, termed a disease.

Perhaps it was time to move on. If he got back into the old crowd, he'd be lost. But who else did he know? Where else had any meaning for him? A new start? More like a dead stop.

A dog barked from under the trees below the bridge. Big dog. There was a path you could walk by the river. Before the mine closures the water ran black eleven months of the year. In August it ran clear. It sparkled.

He caught a whiff of someone's cooking on the wind. Strange, with no house near. Home cooking – whose home? He wondered what smells were made of, and where they went; did they ever disappear wholly, or were they forever diluted, spread far and wide, just so you'd no longer notice? But always there. Was a smell made of atoms or…?

The young woman had come that day from a church, one of the happy-clappy sort. A Sunday, then. People said she wasn't native to the town, hadn't lived here long. Some said she was foreign. Few knew her name. The short newspaper report didn't give it. *She's not the first, and won't be the last*, they repeated – in the pubs and cafés, in the queue at the post-office, at a coffee morning over freshly-baked fruit loaf. After an unsurprising amount of time, nobody spoke of her at all, not even her friend from the crisp factory, the one who'd introduced her to her local house of worship.

The evening stretched before him, celibate, parched. He'd need to stem his ears and avert his gaze if he took the short way home, if he wanted to test his resolve, as this would require passing three watering holes (his *alma maters*, as he once joshingly referred to them) before his turn-off at the end of the High Street. That evening, he'd come the long way, the safe way, down past the school, across the show-field, then skirting the abandoned church, followed the cracked and weedy path by the empty industrial units, to eventually reach the bridge. Out of sight, out of mind. Short cuts could lead to distaster, or worse.

If he risked the short way, would one of the *Blossom Hill Club* collar him as he passed by on the pavement? Outside, with a fag in one hand, a large Merlot in the other: they'd spot him from a hundred paces: *Donkey Dave, Crusty Mary, Dapper*

Lionel (DL for short), or one of the numerous others; so many names, most unreal, bleared faces, woozy vacant grins over forgotten conversations that seemed to mean so much at the time. He knew nothing about them really, nothing concrete. Each one getting sicker, year on year, looking older than their parents, some of them, back living with them, too. The feet getting painful to walk on. The skin yellowing, tiny veins corrupting. Inner damage, unseen for now. Mum calling them down for breakfast, sick buckets by the bed.

At least he'd avoided that – a return to his boyhood bedroom, not that they'd have made him overly welcome beyond a long weekend, at best. 'This is our time now,' his mother had said, whilst planning a mini-cruise of the Balearics. 'Our time, mine and your father's.' He never asked them for money. They never offered. Tough love is still love.

He really ought to give them a call. They might be worried, what with him having been away. Although there were no messages on the answering machine on his return. No post either, other than stuff from the social, and about a hundredweight of pizza leaflets. It'd been a rush job, the rehab', arranged by his key-worker, Courtney (parents jazz fiends, apparently). A six-week holiday from life, but with no escape from reality, somewhere in deepest Gloucestershire.

A big old house, like going back in time. Walled gardens. Mature trees. The pleasant mustiness of his high-ceilinged room. Gurgling pipes. Echoes from a past. All walks (and stumblers) of life. The disease is no respecter of persons, as they say. All the cute phrases, the jargon, that batted around his head, to the point it seemed he and his compadres had learnt a new secret language, one by which they'd recognise each other on the *outside*.

Not that he was cynical about it all, or else he'd have refused to go. *Live in the day* – that was one piece of advice he could relate to, could actually practise, one to hang your coat on.

He'd tried making a few friends at Yarbury Hall, and most people were nice enough, after an initial slow thaw – shakes, tears, abdominal pains, the trench of depression, a sense of total deadness, most of which was caused by withdrawal, so they were told. Some went deep into themselves, grew invisible, others became effusive, challenging, some were almost religious in their bright adherence to the principles being foisted upon them; some were old hands at the stint, were welcomed back like honoured guests.

He might have refused, or thrown the towel in early, but after all, his dole was based on being *receptive* to treatments offered, so underneath, there was always more than a little duress. More tough love. A nudge in the right direction.

When the last day came, only one attendee, Michael, gave him his number (not that he'd given his to anyone). He'd not used it yet. But it might come to that, whatever the therapists counselled. The doctors, therapists, whatever the hell they were, constantly warned against co-dependency, and what might seem at first a cosy and mutually-sustaining connection can, over time, turn into a devastating trap for both of you.

Subtly, then not so subtly, you weaken each other's resolve, you project, you falsely rationalise, you give each other licence, you rebel and conspire until the whole edifice of your sobriety collapses in a piss-smelling doorway at midnight on a wet Tuesday.

The other saying he'd taken away, and which was now etched into his psyche, was: *It gives you wings but takes away the sky.* An eloquent way, he'd thought, to describe his drug of choice, except he never really considered it a *drug* per se, more a way of life. Who didn't drink? Just bores or religious nuts. He looked up into his own sky, the one that was losing its light, minute by minute.

A car came over the bridge at great speed. It was the music that made him turn, if you could call it music. The dulled hollow thud thud thud. Then the overloud engine, primed to be as raucous as possible. This car, small and white with blacked-out windows, suddenly there, a menace. The man immediately sensed four people inside, but if pressed later couldn't say why. It had come to a sudden screeching halt directly opposite where he stood, on his side of the road. Ten feet away at most. The stench of burnt rubber drifted across. The relentless bass thud came from deep within the vehicle, claimed to be its nature, its cold soul. No voice, no other instrument, just that primal sound, dark and foreboding, like a terrible dead heartbeat.

He turned back to look over the valley, willing himself inconspicuous, small, of no threat and of no interest. His lips twitched a silent plea for the car to move off, now they'd had their *fun*. They wouldn't be after directions, that's for sure.

No other car on the bridge now, from either direction, and no pedestrian in sight, as if the bridge belonged to the white car alone, some malevolent troll for our technological age.

A wild yet perfectly reasonable thought struck the man. Might the occupants pile out suddenly, rush him, and toss him head-first over the railing? Four young thugs could do it without much of a problem. Such things had happened. He'd read about one such case on a London bridge. Two young men, tipsy law students, were set upon one night by a large group street rats. The students were both beaten, stabbed, then heaved over the side, to plummet into the freezing dark waters of the Thames. One, amazingly, survived. Things happened. And here, now, who would see? It'd be assumed he'd done it by choice, topped himself, took a dive.

A steadier voice guided him. Just turn slowly, and whatever you do, do *not* look at the car, then move away across the bridge, one safe step at a time, in the direction it'd come from, down to the roundabout at the bottom. There, where a main road is, flag someone down, if necessary, and the white car would need to throw a U-turn to follow, would then be on the opposite side. Distance matters. Creating necessary distance. It saves lives. These calculations pulsed through his mind at alarming speed.

The thudding bass grew marginally louder. The man quarter turned, and in his peripheral vision saw that the front passenger window was now half lowered. There was a pale oval, a face, he presumed, wearing some kind of hat or hood. The man would later describe it as an empty face.

It was now or never. He made to move off, and then they threw it, the driver or the front passenger, he couldn't be sure. It landed by his left foot. The window glided up, once more muting the sound from within, and the white car tore off at an absurd speed, nearly losing control as it careened around the roundabout on the town side of the bridge. He watched it till he could see it no more. The roaring of the straining engine eventually died away too.

He looked down. His first impulse was to kick it away, into the gutter. Disgust rose in his throat. But instead he stooped and picked it up with a trembling hand, as though it were a grenade that might at any moment go off, as though it were possibly live. The sides were sticky. The fall hadn't broken it. It wasn't a brand he'd drunk before. The dregs still lay at the bottom. He held it up to catch what light there now was. Then he did a thing he immediately regretted – he smelt it.

That smell, warm and slightly sour as it was, brought back so much. A litany of release-fuelled insanity, a montage of lights and faces, whisperings and raucous bellowing, mad nights, madder days, waking up God knew where, to start over, get a drink down, bring it up, then another that stays down somehow to stop the shakes, achieve a semblance of humanity. Find the joy again.

By and large, he wasn't much of a home drinker, or bench drinker, or a secret bottle in the overcoat drinker. He needed sociability. He needed communion. And his church was the pub. It all started with that deep need, to connect, to have someone to talk to, although he was happy enough listening, collecting stories for his own use. And he needed the lubricant, it worked its magic, and transformed a dull wet weekday into a palace of charm, danger; life was rendered a theatre, playing out some kind of fractious and endless romance, some serious farce.

And it wasn't about making him brave with women, although it worked well enough with a certain type of woman – the type that drank too, or if not that, the type that was attracted to a man slowly destroying himself. And with these potential partners, who almost never became such, he needed the buzz to keep it alive, the buzz or the dullness, to maintain belief in his interest in them, and prop up his fragile faith that they were interested in him. That they might care what he said, thought, dreamt.

He closed his hand tight around the neck of the bottle, as if choking off its life. He closed his eyes. In less than ten minutes he could be in a bar he knew, where he was known, accepted, where some of the old crowd were sure to be. The men, and some women, who'd welcome him back like a lost brother, a returning soldier, like some wise, once-dead hero. And without judgement, without the wrong sort of questions, as if he'd only just left for a slash. He'd pick up where he left off. Oh yes. And the river of laughter, that sweet lack of focus, those rolling words, and the glazed and loving eyes, that might darken, or sullen, but always willing to sparkle anew. His dedicants – his métier – his tribe; most were the soul of tact, where and when it mattered. His core.

The mouth of the bottle was an inch from his lips, offering a hollow kiss. That another man had drunk from it, perhaps even spat in it, didn't register. He was just about to tip the last half inch of liquid onto his tongue when he saw what he'd later describe to his sister, his GP, the police, to anyone who'd listen as a pulsing of energy about six feet away from him along the bridge. By the rail. Simply there, hovering, intense, colourless. The man moved level to it, yet kept his distance. Directly below, at the bottom of one of the struts, he noticed a loop of some pale material tied round. And undeniably, above this, in a kind of almost circle, the pulsing clear shape that was made of the air yet denser, richer. He stared, and the shape simultaneously drew and repelled him. He thought he might cry out – couldn't. Felt the prick of tears, but they didn't emerge. Now angrier, thickening, now an orb, yes, an orb of vibrant disturbed energy. Not essentially bad, not definitely a threat, yet in turmoil, spinning, jerking, twisting and reform-ing, as though it did not want to exist, yet was made to. In pain, one might say, in great distress. Trying to tear itself to nothing, to formlessness.

The man turned to face the road, refusing the entity behind him. This wasn't a symptom of withdrawal. Such visual dis-turbances had dampened down weeks back. This was for him alone, a revelation perhaps, or an opening on to fresh terror.

Still no cars or vans or bikes. No pedestrian, no solitary walker, nothing, like the beginning or end of some dystopic film.

In the distance, he heard a train, offering small comfort.

The orb pulled at his back, willed him to engage, to approach the barrier. Of a sudden, he twisted 180 degrees and launched the near-empty beer bottle at its centre. It passed right through the vortex, then continued to sail cleanly, as if in slow-motion, between two upright struts of the railing, something he couldn't have achieved if he'd tried a thousand times. Over the edge it flew, down into the dark valley without a sound from its falling, to rest among the trees, roots, bushes, the foliage-thick darknesses, where night creatures were already stirring, where their obscure lives held significance.

The man approached.

The orb of energy was no more, as if a bubble had been pricked, as if it had never been. The man spoke aloud, hand gripping the rail, as he gazed down at the drop. *I'm losing my mind. Maybe drinking was the only thing that kept me together. And crazy as it might seem, it gave me identity. People* knew *me. They enjoyed me. Their faces would light up when I came into the bar. I could tell some rare stories. I could. I became a performer then, all shyness gone, I felt alive then. But now, for the sake of some temporary health or whatever, I've got to shun all that brightness, all that mad love. To slink about in the sober shadows, for what and to where? Back to some poxy damp flat, keep trudging those 12 steps, circling my own grave. Sober and dead in life. Still governed by alcohol forever, still trapped, but in a different way. Sick forever, always on the watch out for a breach in the wall, in a wall that I can't even see. The essence drained out of me.* He looked down. *Would it be so bad?*

The canopy of trees waved in the dim light, colour hanging on just. The trees in motion like a woman's long skirts as she walked. *Would it be so bad?*

His head was heavy and it dragged him forward a little. How heavy the head can be. Was it a new head he was after, or a new heart? How exhausting to start over, and for who? For whose sake? If only he'd had a child, or a woman who needed him. Or something that needed him clear and strong and purposeful.

That Tarot card came to mind, the one he'd drawn earlier that day. The deck was a present from his sister, who'd got into stuff like that after the miscarriage. That image – the burning hut, and outside a broken sword on the ground. Malice. Slander. Undermining. *Watch your back* - the little book that came with the deck had advised this. But the threat, the draw, this time, was in front not behind. It was one drop or the other, each day everyday. *Live in the day.* How the bland ease of that statement now soured in his mouth.

He felt in his jacket and pulled out a piece of green paper. Michael's number – a neat hand, a smiley face. The man on the bridge had no mobile, could not bear the things, a bane of modern life, people lost in those tiny screens, not listening, not receiving, not even looking where they were going – bizarre and sickening, and yet they all did it, grinning into those little black boxes.

If he made it back to the flat that night, he'd make the call. 'Any time of day or night – 24/7,' Michael had said. 'You don't have to speak. Sometimes the connection's enough. This is something I *know*.'

He put the piece of paper back, checked its placing like a high-value note.

The silkily moving branches, the gentle and ceaseless rustling, a world unto itself, got him lost for a minute. It was like the sea, no, more under the sea, so inviting, so natural, so like a soft green bed, so why not?

A few cars went by on the bridge, the world had returned, but the man paid it and them no mind, they barely registered.

Again the smell of cooking on the wind, a spiciness. It flared his hunger. 'Eat regularly and as well as you can afford.' Guy, one of the Group Leaders, had offered this nugget of advice during one sunny afternoon session, as dust particles drifted down through the quiet air of the room. 'Give yourself little treats when you can, a new shirt, a good steak, or veggie alternative, a trip to the zoo or the pictures, whatever floats your dinghy, cos like that daft advert says, *you're worth it!*' Some of them had laughed, but the man on the bridge hadn't, if anything he'd felt like weeping. Wasn't the lake of beer, the tankers of cheap wine, the bathfuls of whisky he'd consumed across nigh on twenty years the ultimate treat? The elixir that made people and places better than they were? The treat that took more, eventually, than it ever gave. That soft-feathered self-obliteration *that gives you wings but takes away the sky.*

The trees down there. Something in the branches. Not a thing. An outline. His mouth began to sag, he wiped his knuckles across it. Why all this? An outline in all that dark moving mass. The shape, this time, of a woman, reavealed then occluded, then shown once more as the branches threshed. Like a picture lit then unlit. A stretched-out body in the canopy, falling. No, not falling, in suspension. Arms thrust out, hair billowing. Perfect balance, in its element. Borne aloft – part of the trees and distinct from them. A cousin to them.

The man crossed himself, a thing he'd not done for thirty years. How his father might smile at that. The late-night conversations they'd had, with him on the brink of manhood. Belief, faith, what comes after, what before. Never so close as then, not earlier or since, in their almost passionate disagreement and burgeoning respect, their separation and simultaneous convergence, as men.

He studied the moving branches. Tried to write her onto them. She was gone again. He ached to see her. His lady of the bridge. He waited and watched. Dark falling heavier, sticking to the skin of his face. Sounds of the town in the mid-distance, everyone's night underway. A high voice pierced the thrum of it.

At last, he stopped waiting. He'd had the gift and would take it as such, as he had Michael's number. He smiled to himself, and for once it was without bitterness, without self-blame.

Straightening, he began walking home the way he'd come. The long way.

Livestock

Valerie O'Riordan

It was a gale of a Hallowe'en, the day I met Lou-Lou Foley, the wind creaming scum off Fernilee Reservoir and spitting it all over the Goyt Valley, skitterings of bonfire smoke whipping from the Buxton hilltops. When I pulled into the farm, Foley's windows were dark, but I knew where I'd to go: I parked by the gate as usual, in Pa's old spot, and trundled the tank just like he'd always done, across the muck, into the calving shed.

There was the heifer, eyeballing me. Hattie Foley. Friesian. Earmark FOL-79. Stocky, I thought. Shoulders like a prop forward and a mean lip. *A fuckin berserker*, Bernie had said on the phone, *but a top little breeder, I'll warrant*. He'd pinned her in the stocks, an iron bar clamped down over her neck so she couldn't back off: instead she lashed her tail and stamped.

'You think this is the bad part?' I muttered. 'Girl, wait.'

I pulled a labeled straw from the tank's bath – *0.5ml of the*

North's Finest Bovine Semen! – and dunked it in my Thermos. Forty seconds. *Tick-tock*: I folded my arms. Little Cheryl Reyniss, the kid I got in to babysit Tilly if I'd to work weekends or evenings, had looked disgusted when I'd explained my job: 'What,' she'd gone, 'like, sticking your hand up a cow's *arse?*' She wasn't wrong: if I'd been a cow, I'd have gored me soon as look at me.

Thirty-nine, forty: out with the straw. I snipped off the tip, snapped the stick into the insertion gun, the glove over my wrist, and slicked on the gel. What you do is this: you slip your slithery hand into the animal's cavity. Fight the clampdown and hunt for the cervical lip, then feed in the nozzle with the straw until you reach the uterine mouth, and then you squeeze the plunger: *bull's-eye!* The juice dribbles out – a hundred and twenty pounds' worth, twice my fee – and ten months later, there's your investment: staggering, slobbering, and head-butting the walls.

Hattie snarled as I mounted the fence, the gun tucked under my armpit. I swung one leg over the top rail. 'Brace yourself, Hats,' I said, and that's when, from inside my jacket pocket, my phone rang. *Dring-dring*, at top volume: *Cheryl*, I thought, because who else ever called anymore? *For fuck's sake* –

The heifer buckled round and kicked. Her rear hoof skidded off my hip; I went *oof*, and toppled backwards off the gate. Landed shoulder first in a crusted cowpat – which burst – and the gun clattered away, over the concrete, under the fence, into the pen. I'd barely time to swear before Hattie, gums bared, ears flattened, cocked her foreleg and stamped: out leaked the juice. *No*, I thought, *no, no, no*, and the heifer let out a triumphant bellow.

'Whoa!' A girl. 'Are you, like, okay?'

A girl? I sat up: a Foley. Fourteen-ish, thickset in a duffel coat and harem pants, and striking, despite her dad's lumpy nose and his feathery ginger hair – and there was me, mortified, dung down one sleeve, hay pasted to the other, sprawled on the floor like a dumb-fuck drunk. Some professional I was. Some adult.

'Are you the A.I. person?' She looked doubtful. 'Daddy said someone was coming in from Manchester?'

'Yeah,' I said, 'that's right, that's me,' and I shifted sideways, as if that would conceal the damage: the splintered gun, the remains of the straw, Hattie's spluttering and spleen.

The girl sucked her bottom lip. 'Can I ask if you're finished?'

'Uh.' I glanced around. 'Well.'

I was pretty sure I *was* finished: once Bernie Foley found I'd wasted his straw – his money, his time – I'd be properly screwed: he'd blacklist me and I'd lose half Pa's client list. *Our* client list. Pa'd go ballistic. And Bernie would find out, wouldn't he, because now the daughter had seen the mess, she'd rat me out. Why wouldn't she? And what then? *You're a fuck-up, Sal*, I thought, Pa's words, *once a fuck-up, always a –*

'Because, like, if you *are* done, I'm kind of looking for a lift?'

I blinked. 'A lift?'

'To, like, Stockport?' She was twiddling her coat buttons.

Her nostrils were raw, flared like the heifer's. 'I've got this – *thing* I have to do, and I sort of can't ask my – so I thought, if it's on your way? Maybe?'

'Maybe,' I echoed. But I felt suddenly hopeful: I was thinking, *tit for tat, love*. If she wanted to steal out to do her *thing*, to get drunk or go gigging or hook up with whatever toxic little shite she was afraid to bring home to daddy, well, okay, but it wasn't *my* thing – so she'd have to make it worth my while. Wouldn't she? Aiding and abetting and all that – I stood up.

'Right,' I said. 'And what's your old man going to say about that? He's my client, remember.'

'But he won't know,' she said. 'He's up the top paddock – they all are, with the bonfire. If we go now –'

'If we go now,' I interrupted, 'you're saying nothing about *this*.' I indicated the broken gun. 'Like, I mean *nothing*. You get it?'

You get it: what was I, Al Capone? I felt myself blush – why would she take me seriously? I wasn't even ten years her senior, I was splattered with cow-shit –

But she was nodding: 'Sure,' she said, 'totally. Like, absolutely.'

Absolutely. I felt myself preen; I *was* a motherfucking gangster! A sonofabitch, in fact, like Tilly's dad, Charlie – though if I had been Charlie, I thought, I'd have bargained a blowjob into the terms, too, and then I'd have driven off without her anyway, and fuck the consequences.

However.

I bent to shovel up the evidence: the gun, the straw, and

then I spat on my hand, Pa-style, and stuck it out. 'Deal,' I said, and she shook.

*

Five minutes later and Pa's old Fiesta was rattling down the Goyt Road: there were the cities massed in the grey distance, Stockport, Manchester, Salford, fireworks popping over all three like cartoon tweetie-birds, and me powering down the country lanes like Bernie Foley was coursing us down in his combine harvester, bawling *that's my fuckin daughter!*

His daughter, though, didn't seem at all buzzed; she just flumped in the passenger seat, picking at the seatbelt's frayed threads like we hadn't just pulled off the most cunning jailbreak in all of bloody Derbyshire. Well, I thought, *I* was having fun, and I wasn't letting it just fade away: when was the last time I'd gotten to do anything even remotely interesting? So I tried to get her chatting – I thought, even, that we could end up mates.

'Well,' I said, 'so my name's Sal?'

A pause. 'What? Oh,' she mumbled. 'Louise. Lou Lou.'

'Nice,' I said. 'Lou-Lou. So. Off out tonight, is it? Seeing your bloke, or – ?' I said this dead lightly, like it didn't at all matter that I hadn't gone out in over a year, that I'd probably never get out again, that *my* bloke didn't return my calls or pay any –

'Nah.' She was looking at the floor, at Pa's old newspapers that still lined the passenger footwell: *The Racing Post, The News of the World.* A girl in a bikini straddling a racehorse – I felt myself redden again. 'I've just this, like, thing to check out, is all.'

'Right,' I said. 'Yeah. Me too.' Like, reheated chicken dippers, ketchup and half a bottle of Tesco's Value Chardonnay while the baby sicked down my front. I'd checked my messages when we'd gotten back to the car: Cheryl had left a series of texts saying they'd *RUN OUT OF NAPPIES!?!?!* Well, I didn't know what she thought I was supposed to do about that. The road down from Foley's was a deep cleft between limestone walls, brambles clumped with sheep's hair, plastic-wrapped bouquets and memorial cards piled up at each S-bend and phone lines jammed through gaps in the rock like tooth floss between blackened molars. There wasn't a Tesco Express in fifteen miles – just crags and trackways, skies so low you'd get soaked just standing up.

Now Lou-Lou's phone beeped. 'Ugh,' she said, and tapped out a reply; it beeped again. 'Prick,' she muttered, and then, to me, 'sorry.'

'S'all right,' I said. 'Boyfriend?'

'Not *even*.' She tucked her hands under her thighs. 'He can piss off,' she added, and I grinned; 'Here,' I began, 'I'll tell you about *my* fella,' but she'd turned away; she'd leaned her head against the side-window and shut her eyes.

Jesus, I thought, *fine*, and I tightened my grip on the steering wheel. *Suit yourself, bitch.*

Whaley Bridge, Disley, Hazel Grove – as the hillsides crumbled, the suburbs shot up, all beauty salons and no-win-no-fee immigration appeals solicitors and builders' merchants. And, as usual, I got caught up in playing *Things I Should've Fucking Well Done With My Life Instead* – this time it was nail technician or travel agent or joiner – so that by the time Lou-Lou lunged forward and rapped on the dash, I'd almost forgotten her and I nearly screamed.

'There!' She banged again. 'There, look – that's Stepping Hill, isn't it? The hospital? Pull in, can you?'

I didn't question her; I just braked. She'd already spoilt whatever fun I might've gotten out of the drive, so now I wanted her gone – I wanted to get home, twist open the own brand vino, and sulk. Immediately, she popped her seatbelt; she'd opened the door before I'd even time to fully stop the car: 'Hey!' I went, startled, pissed off, 'careful, yeah?'

But she just hopped out without so much as a *thanks* or a *see you later*; she was loping towards the building marked Outpatients, her Parka flapping out behind her, the back of it blotched with a dark, crookedly circular stain.

'Hey!' I yelled, properly angry now, 'Lou-Lou! *Louise!*'

She didn't turn. *Wench needs a right good fucking thump*, I thought, and then I was looking down at the upholstery where she'd been sat, and it was stained, too. Now, I wasn't precious about the car – it was a banger, it was as old as me, Pa had left it, literally, to rot – but neither was I looking to have it trashed by strays: it was bad enough with Tilly's puling and pissing. I fingered this new mark in disgust – damp. Morbidly, almost absently, I lifted my hand and sniffed. Blood.

Blood: my stomach clenched, then I was up and out of the

car, banging on the roof and yelling, 'Lou-Lou, wait! Do you hear me – *wait*, for fuck's sake!'

But an ambulance screeched past, drowning me out, and by the time it had parked, she was out of sight. Of course she was; and why should she wait? Who was I? Nobody! But I couldn't just let her disappear: broken straw or no broken straw, if Bernie Foley found out I'd driven away and left his kid in this state, he'd –

Fuck, I thought, and I wrenched the car around to Long Stay; I battled with the Pay & Display machine for a lifetime until it finally hawked out a ticket, and then I ran to Outpatients and gibbered at the porters, 'My, uh, my friend, please, she's bleeding –,' until they steered me towards the lifts.

Up, up, then left, and left again. *Antenatal.* The bruises from my fall in the shed were kicking in now, and I was moving at a gimpy trot past empty gurneys and stupefied, loose-bellied women toting drip-stands; the air tasted familiar, soaked Pampers, and the paintwork was bile-coloured, and the tannoy (*Mr. Gibbins to NICU!*) failed to drown out the screaming from the delivery suites. Abruptly, I was in two places at once: I was here, and I was in the other hospital with Tilly still ripping her way out; Charlie was gone looking for a Coke machine, and I was gagging on the rubber tubing for the Entonox, vomit sliding down my chin –

Christ, Sal, I thought, woozily, *get a grip.*

Through a set of swing doors, and there she was. A midwife escorting her into a consulting room.

'Louise!' I skidded across the tiled floor. 'Lou-Lou!'

She turned. She'd lost the coat – in the thin blue jumper, her belly swelled out clearly, and below the hem, the cotton trousers were definitely bloodied. Her face was ghostly. She clutched her bump and went, 'Oh. Hey.'

But she didn't approach me, and I didn't know how to approach her, and so the midwife just nodded briefly at me and hustled Lou-Lou away through the door. And then the room seesawed: somebody pushed me into a knobbly plastic seat, my head was being pressed between my knees, a voice was yelling: '– drink of water, *now!*'

*

The wait dragged on hours. I switched my phone off so that Cheryl wouldn't keep hassling me, and then I tried to get comfy, but the woman who'd forced a warm bottle of Evian down me had pulled up her t-shirt to 'air herself out', and I could see her exposed belly convulsing; groggily, I'd gotten up, waved her off, went to pace the main corridor instead. Mostly, I was wondering how Lou-Lou done it. I remembered reading up last year on these pills you can get sent from Ecuador or Mexico, how you'd angle a coat-hanger, what kind of a fall it'd take. In the end I'd made an appointment in a clinic in Manchester, but I'd not had the gumption to actually go in, and Charlie had walked off in a temper – I was *a spiteful fucking cunt*, did I know that? So I'd ended up on Antenatal after all: I remembered my old housemate sending me in a gift-wrapped packet of mammoth sanitary towels (the same girl that'd made me move out when I'd failed the pregnancy test), and Charlie checking my stitches after I'd begged him not to, texting his pals that they'd *done a right fucking Frankenstein down there*. And, hazily, Tilly, a hairy, chomping wodge of limbs and gums with Charlie's sunken eyes and my downturned mouth. I must have held her, I knew they made you hold the babies, but I didn't remember anything like that that: I remembered later, living back in Pa's, slouching about in Ma's baggy old smocks, sweating nights over the council housing application and going out on jobs with Pa each morning, Tilly wailing in the back. And Charlie: Charlie ringing up to demand a christening service, Charlie saying no of course he couldn't fucking take her for the fucking weekend, Charlie telling me he'd met somebody else, all right, so could I just ever back the hell off?

But Lou-Lou, she'd gotten away with it, hadn't she? *Bitch*, I thought, pacing, *bitch bitch bitch*, though I wasn't too sure whether I meant her *(fuck her)* or me *(what was wrong with me?)* By the time she finally emerged, anyway, I was sticky, worn out with guilt and annoyance, and fed up. They'd cinched her into these baggy blue hospital scrubs, her own dirty trousers bundled in her arms. She walked draggingly; she didn't look up when I said, 'You ready, then?'

'She'll be sore,' said the midwife, 'and she's exhausted, see? So no driving, no lifting, and give her these, it's on the box, and tell her to call her G.P. if there's any developments.

Though I think we're all done, love,' she added, and patted Lou-Lou's arm.

Lou-Lou didn't move, so I took the tablets, shoved them into her hand. 'So,' I said, 'I mean, you mean it's all, you know – gone? I mean, done?'

The midwife didn't answer; she just squeezed Lou-Lou's shoulder. 'You rest, now,' she said, 'you hear me?'

Lou-Lou shrugged her off; she trudged wordlessly towards the lifts. I chased after her – again – and ushered her around to the car park where I had to buckle her in and even close her door. I slammed my own door, too. Well, I was irked, wasn't I? She could've at least acknowledged me: I mean, if I'd pissed off, she'd have been left shivering at a bus stop – if there even *was* a bus going her way – or stuck back at the farm still, bleeding out on the straw like some bolloxed heifer. I'd helped her – *saved* her, maybe – and I'd thought we might be, like, friends, but all I was getting in return was the fucking grumps. I started the car, and it stalled; I'd flooded the engine. It took me three goes to get us down the exit-ramp. And then – after I'd already automatically signaled and turned north towards home – I realized that I'd no idea where I was meant to be going. Back to Foley's? Or to her bloke's, wherever that was, or to a mate's? A mate's parents, even; she was just a kid, after all, wasn't she? *Shit*, I thought: it's not like I could bring her back to my damp flat, my colicky child. I mean, I hardly wanted to go there myself.

Plus, she was weeping.

Oh God, I thought.

'Uh,' I said, 'so – you're all right, now, yeah? I mean,' when she didn't answer, 'you'll be all right, hey?' And I reached over and prodded – patted – her shoulder. 'All's well that ends well!' I cringed: I sounded like my old school guidance counsellor.

But she'd looked up. 'What?'

'Well,' I said, 'you know. Back to normal, no harm done, that sort of –'

'Oh my God,' she said, 'you're like Daddy. I *wanted* –,' she stopped, rubbed her eyes: the skin beneath them was puffing up, her nose was streaming. 'Oh, forget it,' she mumbled, 'it's not like any of it even matters anymore.'

The fuck, I thought. Then: *she'd not – ?* She'd *wanted* it?

So now I'd no idea what to say; I wanted to go, *don't be thick, love*, or *you've no fucking clue*, but she'd turned back away from me again, and this made me furious: as if any part of this whole mess was my fault! She'd not told me anything, I'd had to guess – she was a child, for fuck's sake! I wanted to drag her back to the flat after all, to thrust Tilly at her and go, *there! Swapsies! Knock yourself the fuck out!* And of course I felt guilty, too – she was a kid, she wanted a cuddle or a fucking inspirational speech, but that wasn't me, I was stiff and angry and seventeen different sorts of screwed up, and what was I supposed to do now?

I swung onto the ring road. I'd lap the city. That was a good one; it calmed me down, it settled Tilly when she was freaking out, it'd buy us time. So in silence, then – hostile or despairing or whatever it was – we swung up past Denton and Droylsden. I stared at the hubcaps, the dead pigeons and smashed traffic cones that littered the hard shoulder, the headlights in the oncoming lanes that smeared into a single savage *whoosh*, the outward signs that leered at me, going SHEFFIELD, IKEA, AIRPORT! *Do it*, I thought, like I did every time: *just go*. And it seemed like if I *was* going to do it, then I'd surely do it now – like, the day was already a catastrophe, so why not cut my losses and hightail it south? But I couldn't, no more than I'd dared to run out of the hospital in my paper gown while the nurses bathed Tilly. I just kept circling. And when we veered back round to Stockport, I pulled off the motorway and took the Buxton Road east.

*

Lou-Lou's parents' place was a thirty-acre spread overlooking Cunning Dale, a Derbyshire gritstone valley that sloped, Pa always said, with heather and yellow rattle, cowslips, red flowering quince, mint leaf beetles, froghoppers and wax-clad ramblers – but all I'd ever seen was flinty land, damp and wind-blasted. Now I passed fields of scraggly, darkening farmland. A spidery copse of yew. A tractor dumped on a waterlogged terrace, the crow-pecked corpse of a John Doe flapping airless from a cross. On the shoulder of the road, before the last turn-off, a pair of hobbies ripped the sinews from the flattened remains of a small dog. And high above the road – in Bernie's upper paddock – the Foleys' Hallowe'en bonfire, haloing the entire ridge, miniscule figures leaping manically about before it. Sparks shot from the neighbouring trees.

I parked, again, in the muddy swamp by the gate, in front of the still-dark house: I undid Lou-Lou's strap, I pushed open her door.

'Well,' I said. 'Here we are.'

She didn't look at me; she staggered noiselessly into the gloom, clutching her bloodied clothes, and vanished around the side of the farmhouse.

I slumped back into my seat and let out an actual hiss of relief, like a valve had been released: *thank fuck that's over.* Though actually I still felt uneasy – like, where'd she gone? What if she kept bleeding? Weren't her parents about? *But it's not my thing*, I reminded myself; hadn't I my own shit to figure out? So, after a long, silent moment, I restarted the car – but when I went to accelerate, the back tyres just spun. Two pinwheels of wet muck sprayed out behind me, and the engine whined. I whined, too – I tried again, the same thing happened, the car dug into the ground, and I punched the steering wheel. No: *stay calm*, I thought, *just chill* – and I switched on the dome light and looked around for the manual – like it would have even helped – but it wasn't there. *Stupid, stupid*: I slumped back in the seat and whimpered.

Finally, feeling mangled and zombified, I heaved myself out into the darkness. *Fetch somebody.*

'Bernie?' I shouted. 'Lou-Lou – ?'

No reply; the yard flung the words spitefully back: *ooh-ooh.* I tried the house – the front knocker, and then the back door – but nobody answered.

The outhouses, then: a series of low stone huts clustered around the house in a loose crescent. The calving shed, the grain store, and a small, disused milking parlour where Bernie kept the dismantled innards of dead machinery – all empty. Empty but for Hattie, that is, still manacled in her pen, who gaped at me and wheezed: I retreated quickly. No Foleys, just the yowling wind, and the revellers whooping on the hilltop –

I set off up the lane at a blind canter, slurping in and out of potholes in the murk. Blackthorn spurs clawed at me from the dead hedge; the track steepened, and I tripped and fell twice, three times as I lurched from furrow to furrow. I was panting so hard that I'd barely have heard anybody approach, though every time I did hear something – an owl's bawl, a rat's scurry – I cried out. Up, up: a never-ending climb, and here the lane was tangled with rotting undergrowth, a wet sag of matted burdock, ragwort and thistle, my hands and wrists stung with bloody slices. But I could feel the heat of the bonfire, now, and the sky was a toxic orange; I was off-road, and scrabbling at loose clods of earth, shards of smashed boulder, splashing through a muddy brook, and then the ground fell away, pla-teaued: I stopped. Swayed.

The fire: colossal, piping, snapping. A ragged line of men slinging armfuls of earth into its belly, buckets of sludgy, hill-stream silt – one of them turned, a tall figure, his face torn open to the bone, scalp running with blood. Beyond him, lumpen-headed creatures in shredded rags –

I stifled a whimper. I felt dizzy again; I tried to turn, to run, but I crashed into a woman, and she shoved a bucket at me; 'Hurry,' she shouted, but my knees caved, I fell, and the water splashed over my legs.

The wounded man staggered past us, towards the stream, his eyes boggling, red-rimmed; he wiped his forehead with a dirty hand, and the white came away with the red – *paint*, I realized, *grease-paint*. A costume – Bernie Foley, in a costume –

The woman was trying to draw me back from the flames, but I pulled loose; I reeled after Bernie, I went, 'Hey, wait!'

He turned, exhausted, looked at me without recognition.

Help, I wanted to say, *I'm fucked* – and I was pointing crazily down the hillside, I was going, 'Listen –,' but he was turning away, ladling up another half-litre of wet slime, moving off – and what came out of me was: 'Your daughter, man – your fucking *daughter*!'

'My – what?' He turned back; he stared. 'What about her?'

But I'd stopped. The wind had gusted a heavy curtain of the blaze aside, revealing, in the middle of the paddock, crows circling and diving and screaming above the dying trees as coppice of oaks smouldered. Beyond that, the timber fence – the farm's boundary fence – burned: the flames licking out along it in a broken line that arched right over the next ridge, into the neighbouring valley.

'For fuck's sake!' Bernie Foley had seized my arm. He shook me. 'What about her? What *about* her?'

'I don't know,' I whispered. The cows, the Friesian herd, were stepping out through the gaps in the fence where the slats had already collapsed; as I watched – as Bernie started to shout – one by one, they disappeared.

End Times

Maxim Loskutoff

Elli wouldn't let me stop until we'd crossed the line into Utah. She was a nail in the passenger seat – rigid, sharp, her blue eyes darting back and forth between the speedometer and the double yellow lines. Dry rivers of makeup connected her eyes to her chin. Leon lay where I'd put him across the backseat. His chin was propped on a pile of Carlos Castaneda books. Strands of drool hung from the orange spines. His haunches trembled whenever we went over a bump. His glazed, suffering face was fixed on the back of Elli's bare shoulder. We'd gotten most of the blood out of the slate-colored fur on his back but there were still flecks on his pale belly.

Route 89 flanked the scrub brush and dust of Nevada for thirty miles before turning north through Kanab. A half-empty bottle of Popov rattled in the cup holder. Elli lifted it by the neck. 'We might need that,' I said. She paused, considering, and then sipped it anyway. Power lines, suspended from trans-former towers, were strung across the sky as far as I could see. Probably they ran all the way down to Mexico, like bandits.

Kanab only had one gas station, a neat little Sinclair with a scrubbed forecourt and gleaming green pumps. I pulled in, parked. It hardly even smelled like gas, the air was so fresh. A pine forest came right up behind the store. 'Home of the State Champion Lady Rams' read a banner on the window where the beer advertisements should've been. I put my foot on the concrete plinth beneath the pump, swiped my credit card, and lifted the nozzle from its holster.

Elli got out and stretched. Her long torso gave her a snaky, undulating look as she leaned right and left, her arms over her head, her bare feet on the pavement. She walked stiffly to the bathroom at the side of the store, rolling her neck. 'Put some shoes on,' I wanted to yell after her, but I knew she wouldn't. She was free-spirited about germs, money, underwear, and di-rections. Everything else she worried about.

A clump of fur clung to the hem of her orange dress. One of the shoulder straps had fallen. It hovered above her elbow. Clothes had a way of slipping off her frame, unable to dis-guise the girl beneath. My shoulders ached from driving all day, and from carrying Leon.

She came out with a wad of wet paper towels, her face ra-diant with worry. She opened the Sentra's dust-sprayed back door and started dabbing the fur around Leon's wound. We'd doused it in vodka and bandaged it up as best we could with athletic tape and a clean t-shirt from my gym bag. The bullet had gone in through his hip. I wondered if it was a bad place for a coyote to get shot – if they kept any organs back there.

'He'll be fixed up by this time tomorrow,' I said. 'He'll make it.'

Elli didn't answer. She just kept dabbing. Her thin arms were surprisingly muscular. She didn't work out, but she was tense all the time. Even in sleep she ground her teeth. Leon didn't complain about her touching him. He never did; never growled, not so much as a snort. Elli put her cracked lips against Leon's nose. Their eyes met.

A gust of wind came in from the north and I shivered as I replaced the nozzle. We were climbing into winter latitudes. 'Montana,' she'd said, when I'd emerged from the canyon with Leon a bleeding bundle in my arms. She knew a vet there, a friend of her father's. She'd seen him bring a shot wolf back from worse, apparently, and he wouldn't report us to animal control.

'Everything okay out there?' the cashier asked, when I went in to buy some water and chapstick. She was prettier than most women who work in gas stations. Tan, with feather earrings and a mother's worried smile.

I nodded, realizing there was blood dried on my shirt. 'Spilled some coffee.'

Mountains began to break through the desert. Red ones first: mesas, buttes, hoodoos. I told Elli about the time my father took us to Zion. We stayed in a Travelodge in Hurricane. It had HBO, and my brother and I just wanted to stay in the room and watch. My dad got so angry that he broke the TV screen with his fist and we went home two days early. Elli traced triangles on the window with her finger as the yellow-brown landscape blurred by. She wasn't listening. Her lips, wet now with chapstick, were pressed together. Freckles shone through the makeup carelessly dusted on her nose. She was beautiful in a wrung-out, haggard sort of way that I couldn't get over.

Leon peed. It hissed onto the floor, soaking the carpet and empty Styrofoam cups under my seat. The sweet toxic vinegar stink made my eyes water.

Elli turned and watched him struggling to get out of his mess. He knocked two of the books off the seat. His paw flailed the air. His hind leg was soaked, the wet fur matted to the bone. Yellow drops slid down the plastic seat cover onto the floor. 'It's okay,' she said. 'It's okay.'

I rolled the windows down and let the dry air blast my face. We merged onto I-15: four wide lanes running north all the way to Butte. I kept my eyes away from the rearview mirror. In a day or two, three at most, I'd be back home, freshly showered, lying on my couch with a cold beer, watching women's tennis. Brown grass grew through gravel in the median. Semis rattled as we passed them, spitting diesel from their dark underbellies.

An hour went by before Elli spoke. 'He needs food,' she said. 'It'll just make him shit,' I answered.

She looked at me like I was a half-squashed insect.

'I'm kidding,' I said. 'C'mon.'

I took the Nephi exit and drove up and down the quiet Mormon streets, past rows of white clapboard houses with blue trim and lawns mowed down to a military stubble. There was a hardware store, a confectioner's. I didn't know what we were looking for. Leon liked to eat cats, and he liked to eat them when they were still alive. I suggested using catnip as chum to lure one into the car.

'It isn't funny,' Elli said.

We found a shaded parking spot behind The Country Kitchen, between a dumpster and a waxed red Mustang, probably the manager's – some kind of hotshot. I changed shirts, gathered the piss-soaked cups in the old one, and threw the whole mess into the dumpster. Elli cracked the windows. She opened the back door and promised Leon we'd be back soon. I came and stood beside her. I'd need new floor mats, maybe new seat covers. Her head barely crested my shoulder. If she ever left, it was the fresh coral smell of her scalp that would haunt me. 'Be good,' she said, like he was her own son. 'Stay.'

He lifted his head off the books, blinking. His amber eyes were wider than usual, glowing in the short white hair around them. His mouth was clamped shut. He was embarrassed, hurting. When he was happy, his mouth lolled open toothily.

Damn coyote. I reached out to touch his face. He whipped his jaws at my fingers, snapping.

'Goddammit.' I jerked my hand away. He'd bit me once,

when he was just a pup, and I still had two small scars beneath my thumb. He was five times that size now. His incisors were a half-inch long and I'd seen what they could do to a cat's skull. My ears rang. I wanted to hit him. I turned and walked quickly toward the restaurant.

Elli murmured to him, gently shut the door, and followed me inside.

The waitress led us to a booth in the corner. Each of her thighs was as wide as Elli. Her blue apron was stretched tight across her groin like a linebacker's jock. I hoped the Mustang was hers. The vinyl covering the booth squeaked when I sat down. There were paper placemats and a cup of crayons. Elli looked out the window at a gray steeple knifing into the sky. Her blond hair was cut one length all around, at her chin. Her face was drawn and gray at the edges, marked by exhaustion, physically beat, but also lit by it, as if she were becoming more alive.

She ordered a cherry malt and a steak.

'You need food too,' I said.

'I'll eat the potatoes.'

The steeple didn't have a crucifix but it was a church, sure enough. I'd heard somewhere that you had to be a Mormon to go into a Mormon church. I wondered if that was true, and if so, what was inside. I drew Richard Nixon in green on my placemat – all glowering jowls.

The waitress brought the malt on a silver tray. A cloud of whipped cream floated on top. Elli gave it all of her attention. The tendons in her neck stretched tight as she worked the straw. The skin on her right shoulder was sunburned a deep red from the car window.

'Slow down,' I said. 'Your brain will freeze.'

When the glass was empty, Elli folded the straw into a triangle. She filled the triangle with salt – a white pyramid. Dry blood was crusted around her nails.

'He tried to bite me,' I said.

She broke a grain of salt with her thumbnail. 'He's hurt and scared.'

'Well they'd kill him here. All these hunters.' I nodded at the empty street.

Country music was playing softly and the waitress snapped her fingers just once as she pushed through the swinging steel doors into the kitchen. My burger came out separated into components on the plate: lettuce, tomato, onion, bun – all lined up next to the patty. Elli watched me put it together and then she watched me eat. The steak in front of her was shaped like Nevada and just as barren. I could tell she was counting the seconds in her head – *tick, tick, tick*. The waitress was leaning on the counter by the pies, watching me too. I hardly chewed.

When the check came, Elli didn't ask for a box. She just wrapped the steak in a paper napkin and carried it out, dripping, in her bare hand. I left a tip and followed her, smiling apologetically.

The air outside was sharp with the coppery smell of exhaust. Goosebumps rose on her bare arms. A drop of steak juice ran down her calf. It had been hot in Phoenix when we left. Now, dusk was settling over the Wasatch Mountains. The snowy ridges made a jagged pink EKG running north. I put my hand on her shoulder, feeling the bones.

'It was Rod,' she said, opening the back door. 'I know it was.'

I shook my head. 'There's lots of people it could have been.'

'It was Rod.' She held the steak out to Leon. I told her to be careful, but it wasn't necessary. He ate it gently, keeping his teeth away from her fingers. He nodded his head back after each bite, gulping down the meat. Juice clung to his whiskers. He glanced at me, smugly.

'Rod's a fag,' I said. 'They don't have guns.'

Leon finished and licked Elli's hands clean. 'They have cats.'

'Had.' I laughed, despite myself.

Elli exhaled, long and slow, and I pictured myself as a chart inside her head. Two sides: good and bad, with scraps of conversation, things I'd done, memories, posted on either side. The bad side just kept filling up.

'I'm doing this for you, you know,' I said. 'Skipping work, driving all this way. I mean, I care about Leon.'

'Do you?' she asked.

'Of course.' Anger warmed my chest. 'But he's a wild animal.'

She squeezed his skull, massaging the base of his ears. 'So you'd let him die?'

'You know that's not what I meant.' But maybe it was. He'd been trouble since the day we brought him home. He stank up our bed, gnawed the baseboard, shed everywhere. I'd find cat parts strewn around the yard: a paw wedged in the gate, innards on the tomato plants, a half-chewed skull on the welcome mat. He'd start to growl whenever I raised my voice at Elli.

He pressed his long bristly chin into her hands and licked her wrist. 'We're almost there, love,' she whispered. 'Just a few more hours.'

I turned the heat on and we continued north. I held the needle at seventy-five for a while – I didn't know what I'd say if a cop pulled us over – but Elli kept staring at me so I edged it up over eighty. The big empty plains closed around us until the only light was the wedge of the high beams. I was exhausted. My head hurt. The muscles in my thighs ached from climbing up and down the canyon walls, tripping in the dark. Leon had been well hidden in a dugout between two boulders. I'd found him and carried him out. Elli seemed to have forgotten that.

She sat with her feet up on the passenger seat, her arms wrapped around her shins, her thighs against her stomach. Her chin hovered above her knees. The dashboard lights shone hazy and green on her drawn face. Her left eye twitched, the pinched skin revealing the pattern of future wrinkles. We listened to the radio until it crackled and turned to static. I knew there were farmhouses and pastures not far off but it felt like the world could end and we wouldn't know till morning.

Trying to stay awake, I pictured her naked. Right there in the passenger's seat, like she was, except the dress and underwear gone. Her thin muscled arms wrapped around her knees. The skin over her ribs scratched and bruised from clambering through the canyon. Her body folded over itself, pressed together, the color of wheat.

I put my hand on her knee. I let it slide down to where I could feel the rough lace hem of her underwear. She shifted away from me, pushing down my hand and her dress.

Fine, I thought. Fine fine fine.

Salt Lake City was a ghost beneath the freeway: silent buildings forming the uneven steps of a skyline at night, the slow blink of airport lights. The temple, with its turrets and balustrade, looked like a lost castle, stranded on the wrong continent. An American flag hung motionless on a hilltop, lit from below.

Past city limits, the houses gave way to fields lined with huge crouching sprinklers. One of them was on, throwing arcs of mist into the night. Time sped up and skipped forward. I thought of the women I'd known, the places I'd been, bandits, wolves. The car was so warm. My head fell, then jerked upright.

'We have to stop,' I said. 'Get some rest.'

'I'll drive.'

We switched places at another gas station. The clerk watched us through the window, a toothpick rolling between his lips. He was black. Black in Utah. It couldn't be easy. The motel next door was a long low twenty-roomer slung around a parking lot. 'Thunderbird,' read the blue neon sign. I knew the mattresses were probably thin with stained yellow sheets and sharp springs, but I didn't care. I just wanted to stretch out. Leon's eyes gleamed in the rearview mirror. Part of his tongue hung between his teeth, pink as bubblegum.

Elli drove with both hands on the wheel, ten and two. Her lips moved every once in a while. Pursing into an almost kiss, then pulling back over her teeth.

'Does this vet have beds?' I asked.

'At his house,' she said. 'Go to sleep. I'll wake you.'

I let my head roll against the seat. It smelled like fur and piss. The engine hummed beneath me and I imagined giant horses and giant natives, a hundred feet tall, thundering over the dark mountains.

The car was stopped when I woke. We were on the shoulder, a vast plain all around. The headlights were off. Pure black, and above, a field of stars. I blinked, trying to swallow some moisture into my parched mouth. 'Look,' Elli whispered.

Leon was sitting up. His front paws were underneath him, propped unsteadily on the shifting covers of the books. His nose was pushed against the window. His scrawny body – only two, still a puppy – was angled down to where his wounded hindquarters rested on the seat. His eyes were fixed on the waning thumbnail of moon as if it held the answer to all suffering.

The dark southern hills rose and fell like waves. His breath fogged the glass.

He pressed his long gray ears flat against his skull, opened his mouth, and howled. High and sharp, the sound sliced open the roof and carried into the night. He held the note. Piercing. Desperate. It was so loud it hurt my eardrums.

'No,' I said. 'No barking.'

His haunches shook. He slipped and fell against the door.

Elli was twisted around in the driver's seat, stretched toward him, her face contorted, her skin the same color as the moon.

'Where are we?' I asked.

She paused, staring at me. Her bared eyes held something frightening: disgust, maybe, or the beginning of hatred. 'Get out,' she said.

I looked at her blankly. A few strands of her hair stuck to the headrest, straight out beside her, taut with electricity.

'Please. Just give us a minute, alone.'

I fumbled with the door; I kept yanking the handle until she reached across my chest, shouldering me back, and unlocked it. I pushed open the door. The cold night air stung my face. I stood up, dazed, then leaned back into the car. Elli stared at me, her lips pulled tight, the tendons in her neck raised against her skin. Leon's claws scrabbled the plastic seat cover in the back.

'He's going to die,' I said, and slammed the door.

Pebbles crunched beneath my sneakers. I walked away from the highway, down into a ditch, and back up again. I smelled snow, trees. Idaho, maybe. I thought I'd walk until I found a place to fall down. Orion's Belt and The Big Dipper hung at opposite ends of the sky. I couldn't remember any of the other constellations. Just a mess of stars.

The Unthologists

Daniel Carpenter is a London based writer. His fiction has been published by *Unsung Stories*, *The Shadow Booth*, and *The Irish Literary Review*. His podcast, The Paperchain Podcast, was longlisted for a Saboteur Award in 2017 and is currently in its second series.

Elaine Chiew is based in Singapore and London and is the editor/compiler of *Cooked Up: Food Fiction From Around the World* (New Internationalist, 2015). She won The Bridport Prize in 2008 and Elbow Room Prize (2015). She's been named Wigleaf Top 50 Microfiction, nominated for Best of Small Fictions 2016 and shortlisted and long listed in other competitions and awards, including Baltic Residencies, Pushcart, Short Fiction, Mslexia, BBC Opening Lines, Fish International Short Stories, among others. Her most recent stories can be found in *Potomac Review* and *Singapore Love Stories* (Monsoon Books, 2016) which has been shortlisted for the Singapore Popular Choice Awards. She has recently completed an M.A. in Asian Art History from Lasalle College of the Arts (Goldsmiths accr.) and a writer's residency at School of the Arts, Singapore.

Brian Coughlan has a Masters Degree in Screenwriting from NUIG. He has published work with *Toasted Cheese; Litro NY; Storgy; Write Out Publishing; The Galway Review; Bohemyth; The Legendary; Litbreak Magazine; Thrice Publishing Anthology Aug 16; Fictive Dream; The Exceptional Writer; The Ham Free Press; ChangeSeven Magazine; Bitterzoet Magazine; Crack the Spine; and Sentinel Literary Quarterly.*

K.M. Elkes lives and works in the West Country. He began writing seriously in 2012 and has since won the Fish Publishing flash prize and been shortlisted four times for the Bridport Prize. He has also won or been placed in (among others) the Short Fiction Journal Prize, PinDrop Prize, Aesthetica Creative Writing Award, the Prolitzer Prize and the Labello Press International Award. His work has appeared in more than 20 anthologies as well as literary magazines such as *Structo, Litro, Brittle Star and the Lonely Crowd*. His work is part of school curricula in the USA, India and Hong Kong. He is currently the Co-Editor of The A3 Review magazine and is working on his debut collection. Twitter: @mysmalltales.

Tracy Fells lives close to the South Downs in West Sussex. She has won awards for both fiction and drama. Her short stories have appeared in *Firewords* and *Popshot* magazines, online at *Litro New York*, *Short Story Sunday* and in anthologies such as *Fugue*, *Rattle Tales* and *A Box of Stars Beneath the Bed* (National Flash Fiction Day anthology). She was the 2017 Regional Winner (Canada and Europe) for the Commonwealth Short Story Prize and has been shortlisted for the Commonwealth, Fish, Bridport, Brighton and Willesden Herald Prizes. Tracy has an MA in Creative Writing from Chichester University and is currently seeking a publisher for her short story collection. She tweets as @theliterarypig.

Liam Hogan is a London based writer and host of the monthly literary event, Liars' League. His award winning short story "Ana", appears in *Best of British Science Fiction 2016* (NewCon Press) and his twisted fantasy collection, *Happy Ending Not Guaranteed,* is published by Arachne Press. Find out more at http://happyendingnotguaranteed.blogspot.co.uk/, or tweet @LiamJHogan

Maxim Loskutoff's debut collection *Come West and See* was published in May 2018 from W.W. Norton in North America and Albin Michel in France, followed by the novel *Spirits.* A graduate of NYU's MFA program, he was the recipient of a Global Writing Fellowship in Abu Dhabi and the M Literary

Fellowship in Bangalore. He lives in western Montana.

Mark Mayes has had stories and poems published in magazines and anthologies; in particular, the *Unthology* series. *The Gift Maker* a novel, was published in 2017, with Urbane. Mark also likes to write songs.

Jay Merill is published by or has work forthcoming in *A-Minor Magazine, Brilliant Flash Fiction, CHEAP POP Lit, Ellipsis Zine, Entropy, Hobart, Journal of Compressed Creative Arts,Jellyfish Review,The Literateur, Lunch Ticket, matchbook, MIR Online, Storgy, Thrice Fiction* and *Trafika Europe*. She is a 2017 Write Well Award nominee, a Pushcart Prize nominee and the winner of the Salt Short Story Prize. Jay is the author of two short story collections published by Salt – *God of the Pigeons* and *Astral Bodies* - which were nominated for the Frank O'Connor Award and Edge Hill Prize. She is Writer in Residence at Women in Publishing.

Valerie O'Riordan's work has appeared in *Tin House Online, LitMag, The Lonely Crowd, The Mechanics' Institute Review, Fugue, Sou'wester, Litro* and other journals. She is Senior Editor at *The Forge Literary Magazine*.

Gareth E. Rees is the founder and editor of the website *Unofficial Britain* (wwww.unofficialbritain.com), author of *The Stone Tide* (Influx Press 2018) and *Marshland* (Influx Press, 2013).

His work has featured in anthologies including *An Unreliable Guide to London* [Influx Press], *Mount London* [Penned in the Margins], *Acquired for Development By* [Influx Press], *Walking Inside Out: Contemporary British Psychogeography* [Rowman & Littlefield], *The Ashgate Companion to Paranormal Cultures* [Ashgate], and the spoken word album *A Dream Life of Hackney Marshes* [Clay Pipe Music]. He awaits the apocalypse in Hastings with his two daughters and a dog named Hendrix.

Kathryn Simmonds has published two collections of poetry, 'Sunday at the Skin Launderette' (2008) and 'The Visitations' (2013) with Seren Books. Her novel 'Love and Fallout' (2014) is also published by Seren. Her stories and poems have been widely anthologised and broadcast on BBC Radio 4. She lives in Norwich with her family and teaches for The Poetry School.

Hannah Stevens is a writer currently based in Leicester. She writes short stories and flash fiction, and has just completed her first book-length collection. She has a PhD in Creative Writing from the University of Leicester. When not writing, she works part-time in the voluntary sector and also likes to hang out with her house-rabbit Agatha.

Tom Vowler is an award-winning novelist and short story writer living in south west England. His debut story collection, *The Method*, won the Scott Prize and the Edge Hill Readers' Prize, while his novels *What Lies Within* and *That Dark Remembered Day* received critical acclaim. He is editor of the literary journal *Short Fiction* and an associate lecturer in creative writing at Plymouth University, where he completed his PhD. Tom's second collection of stories, *Dazzling the Gods*, was published in January 2018. More at www.tomvowler.co.uk